Red Kelkirkstadt
Torture Magic Novel 3.11 (39)

By Douglas Todt

First Edition (2022)

Chapter One
The Solider on Ice
November 1, 2020

"You continue to, how you say?" asked Golden Bear.

"Study?" offered Geneva, not looking up from her book.

"Work ass off."

She looked up and smiled. They were in an office in the underground cave system where for more than three months now they had been attempting to free a Roman soldier frozen in the ice nearly two centuries earlier.

Special Ops sure led to weird jobs.

The office was much nicer than when Geneva and Golden Bear had arrived in the cave in Siberia on June 20. Although small, Geneva had decorated it with plastic plants, painted the walls mint green, and brought in a white desk. The filing cabinets were still military gray. There was a rug with a pattern of a starfield over the concrete floor and the two side walls had pictures of Lockshire, the deceased bloodhound Geneva had rescued as a teen from drowning in the Atlantic when she first manifested her powers as a teenager.

Geneva sat behind the desk in an orange swivel chair. Golden Bear was leaning against the filing cabinet nearest the door, which opened to Geneva's far left, his right, and the rest of that wall was six-foot tall filing cabinets.

"Me still think translator app just as efficient," said Golden Bear.

Geneva made a face. "They miss subtle dialects. Anyhow, Latin as spoken by a Roman two thousand years ago is far different from the standard Latin passed around today. The app won't pick up the temporal variances." Then with annoyance she said, "I've explained this to you."

"Da." Then he smiled "Me just, how you say?"

"Lazy?" she said, arching an eyebrow.

"Seeker of truth."

She rolled her eyes. Now thirty-four, Ops paranormal agent Geneva Kane was a pretty woman, one that had matured considerably from the snotty teenager that had joined Ops when she was just eighteen. Now she was a mature, attractive, *classy* woman, although not exceptionally beautiful. She had wavy black hair that was straight on top with bangs in front. Her hair draped halfway down her shoulder. Her eyes were bright blue and her face slightly square shaped but attractive. Her smile was cute and occasionally sassy. Her body was not as shapely as some, but she was attractive, with lots of curves, especially her bottom, legs and hips. She was a proper weight for her five-and-one-half-foot frame, but not in great shape — she despised working out but was good with her diet. Today she wore a black, long-sleeve shirt with white cuffs and collar and a picture of a white cat's face over the left breast with a black mini-skirt over black and white hose. Her yellow boots went halfway up the thigh. Geneva loved footwear of all types. The yellow boots were new, and necessary. It was chilly in the cave.

The year had been trying. Although she was a native of Maine, where her mother still lived, she had spent most of the time since mid-June in this cave and the nearby areas of Siberia, trying to free Anthony, the soldier frozen in the rock. Her one trip back to the states had resulted in the disastrous events of the plane crash in August in New Mexico, an event from which she had fully recovered physically. But mentally, she still grieved for her friend and fellow agent Kacie Siu, killed by a robot in the battle.[1]

"We eat dinner soon."

"I have to keep working," she said irritably.

Golden Bear nodded. Since the attack on Portland by the Consortium members led by Calico Kelkirk on September 24, an attack that wiped out two million lives and souls, Geneva had been fiercely intent on freeing the soldier, convinced that was their last viable option of stopping Calico's plans, which had already used the alien Quotient, which fed on human souls for power, as the means of establishing a new colony on Mars.

Geneva was convinced Portland wasn't going to be the end of Calico's mass murders.

Golden Bear prodded. "Food good. I import crab."

She looked up and smiled politely, "Very well. I appreciate the effort. Give me a few minutes."

"Da. Meanwhile, I, how you say?" he asked, pointing towards the bathrooms.

"Use the washroom," offered Geneva.

"Take a whizz."

She nodded as he walked away. Golden Bear was now approximately a century old, but he looked about sixty thanks to a combination of healing spells and glamours, which were how a TM was able to alter his or her base appearance and look older or younger. He was tall and gaunt, but not frail. He emanated power. He had more wrinkles than a mountain range and multiple age spots on his skin. His eyes were icy blue, almost white, and his teeth were dentures. Despite a prominent nose, he was probably attractive in his youth. His hair had mostly vanished, but there was a small, long ring left around the edge of his skull, all white. He was about six feet and eight inches tall, and his arms and legs were skinny. Part of the team that had helped kill Hitler at the end of World War II, Golden Bear was a hero in his native country. He was busy trying to establish a Russian version of Special Operations, but that had suffered a setback

---

[1] See TM 3.9 "Crash and Burn"

in January when it was found Calico and Englehart, the two lead Consortium members, had infiltrated the group.

Wearing wrinkled gray slacks, a white and black checkered shirt, and dirty boots, he looked like someone having just stepped out of a retirement home. Frankly, he looked that way most of the time.

Just as Golden Bear rounded the corridor towards the restroom, part of a very small section of rooms built into the rock years ago by the alien Lexx as part of his plan to free the frozen Roman soldiers, he ran into the man who had been manning the complex for years, the paranormal Igor Kazankov. Kazankov looked a bit like an insect. He was tall and bony, with dark circles around tired brown eyes, unkempt brown hair, and a very oddly shaped jaw. He presently wore a brown sweatshirt over jeans, both very dirty. But despite his looks, he was one of the most powerful channelers either Geneva or Golden Bear had encountered. Most elemental channelers used telekinesis to manipulate the four ancient Greek elements earth, air, wind, and fire. Igor was a variant who could channel a basic force, and in his case that force was the *tachyonic* force. That was the key to their objective, freeing Roman solider trapped in ice . . . that wasn't really ice but in a random tachyon field (RTF).

Igor was normally as expressive as a cardboard box, so the wide-eyed look on Igor's face alarmed Golden Bear, who stopped immediately. "What's wrong?"

"He's awake!"

"Easy, Sir Antony," said Geneva gently as they lay the Roman soldier on a medical bed long-ago prepared for this moment.

"Are you a nurse?" he asked in Latin.

Geneva nodded and responded in perfect Latin, "I will care for you. We are friends. You are far from home."

Antony merely nodded. He was a tall, muscular man with graying black hair, stubble, and a scar above the right eye. Handsome, his Roman soldier's uniform was in tatters. He was wet from the melted ice.

Golden Bear and Igor stayed back several yards. All three of them wore protective masks. The cavern was approximately 1,200 square feet of floor space, hewn out of the rock, similar to the room where they had found Octavious, another frozen solider who died almost instantly on awakening, months ago. There was an office in the corner where Igor spent time monitoring the work of the lasers. The calibration and cutting was precise, thanks to the tech Geneva had brought in, but still extremely difficult.

Igor had arrived in 2014 at the guidance of the alien Lexx, who led the Consortium clandestinely until Ops stopped him in early 2016. This was the site of a battle where Quafara had turned on Quotient in the time of Christ and somehow locked him in the RTF. This froze a person in time and space, as if they didn't exist.

Penetrating it was extremely complex because the RTF was composed of tachyons on a random wave. That displaced space around the object, so as the team penetrated one part, the randomness of the field shifted the entire object and whittled away what had been excavated. Igor's ability helped mitigate that. He could use his channeling of tachyons to keep the random field from displacing his own body and mind and slow the RTF's counter-movements.

And at last, it had paid off.

In Latin, Geneva said to Anthony, "What's the last thing you remember?"

"Did we win?" he asked, either not hearing or ignoring her question. "Is the mad god gone?"

Cautiously, Geneva said, "The battle is over. We're not sure if the God is gone. What's the last thing you remember?"

He looked up at her and coughed. "My sons. Do you know of my sons?"

"What are their names?" she asked.

"Cesar and Douglas."

"They are well," she lied evenly. Realizing he was disoriented, she asked, "Are you in pain, sir?"

Wearily, he sighed. "Only in the soul."

"Are you injured?" she asked, not entirely sure he had understood her question.

He stared a moment and then said, "No. The god blasted us with . . . haze."

"Haze?"

"Yellow haze," he said.

Geneva glanced back at Igor and Golden Bear and said in English, "Zapped in yellow haze. That sounds like Quotient."

"I do not know your words," said Antony.

"Uh, Quotient is the name we have given the mad god," she said quickly in Latin. "May we examine you to insure you are not injured? Sometimes in the heat of battle, wounds are ignored."

"That is acceptable," he said.

Geneva quickly examined him. She certainly wasn't a nurse, but all his vitals seemed appropriate. He looked okay, although he was all wet. Geneva then pulled up a chair and sat to his left. "How many were at the final battle?"

"Dozens. We thought we had the power . . . we were fools . . . fools," he said, clearly despondent. Then he seemed to notice his surroundings for the first time, "Where am I?"

"France," said Geneva, using the Latin term for it.

"Far from the battle?"

"Yes. Where was the battle?"

He referenced two rivers Geneva didn't know. She caught Golden Bear's eye, and he used his phone to check on the location. Meanwhile, she asked him, "Who led the final forces?"

"Pontius Pilate, of course."

"The other side?"

"Why do you ask what everyone knows?" he asked suspiciously. "And why do you were such odd clothes?"

"You are in a strange land, Sir Antony," she said, sounding confident and soothing. She patted his arm. "Our descriptions of the final battle may not match yours. There are no living witnesses."

"I suspected as much," he said grimly. "I was fortunate. When the god began to suck my soul, I fell off a ledge into the river and was swept away."

Geneva frowned. "Who led the other forces?"

"Elkrod and Quafara, of course. Aye, vicious savages."

"Indeed. I have heard of them. You chose to attack them directly?"

"Aye. That was Pilate's idea. He had been exiled nine years prior. Many thought he had been killed or committed suicide, but it was really to gather the army for the final battle . . . Pilate made many a mistake in his life, but in the end, he was a warrior."

"It seems so. How did you propose to stand against the mad God with only a couple dozen soldiers?"

"We had the sword."

She arched an eyebrow. "The sword?"

"This be, how you say? Sci-fi novel?" asked Golden Bear.

Since he was speaking English, Antony just started at him. Geneva politely gestured to him to shut up.

"What sword? Where is it?" she asked Antony in Latin.

Antony began to cough. He didn't notice the alarm in Geneva's face as he said, "Was with me . . . when I . . . fell."

She looked at Golden bear, but he was already searching the area where Antony had exited the ice.

"My sons."

"As I said, they are well."

"They were at the . . . it seems dark in here."

"Antony, can you tell me what happened? Did Quotient survive?"

He now looked very weak and was gasping for air. "He slew many of us . . . the sword brought him down, but that is when Quafara turned on him . . . I don't remember. I just remember him falling . . . like a rock from space . . . then . . . you."

"I understand."

He put a hand on her hair. "You are very . . . lovely."

Then he died.

Golden Bear suddenly cried out, "By the beard of Lenin!"

Geneva closed Antony's eyes and raced to Golden Bear. He had removed a sword form the melted ice. It was long, sharp, and stained reddish brown on the blade. The brown hilt was worn but unstained. He started to reach to touch the blade.

"No, stop!" shouted Geneva.

"What wrong?"

"Look at it. It looks like blood."

"I not get disease. It long dead," he said, a little annoyed he couldn't play with the sword.

"I know, but whatever that substance is might be the key to stopping Quotient. I don't need to you mucking about with it like a kid playing Three Musketeers."

"Da," he said, nodding.

Igor asked Geneva, "What about his body?"

"We'll take care of it."

As he moved away, Golden Bear asked Geneva, "Do all this info, how you say?"

"Help?"

"Give 4-1-1."

She shook her head. "I don't know. It depends what's on that blade . . . I need to get it to Ops for analysis."

"Da, I agree. That take time and they busy. Election in two days."

Sighing, she said, "Well, that's moot anyhow. Dayne has it wrapped up. Heck, even if she were implicated in a child sex scandal, it's too late. There's nothing that can stop her winning the presidency now."

Chapter Two
Election Night
Tuesday, November 3, 2020

"The stars are bright tonight. It makes you hope," said Searly McTaggert to Ashley McMillian as they sat on the front porch of Ashley's family home in Centralia, Washington, at eight in the evening. Crickets serenaded them, getting in some last songs before winter.

Twenty-six-year-old Ashley smiled. She had a fetching little bob cut. Her face was attractive and round, with light blue eyes, brownish and blonde hair, and a body that was purely round in the right places. She had large breasts pushing even her bulky blue sweatshirt, and her gray pants were tight on her shapely bottom. Ashley had one of those bodies that made men drool. She was five-five and a sturdy 140 pounds.

A graduate of Portland State, her parents still lived in Centralia, the main reason Ashley, Thunder, and Searly McTaggert were at the house on election evening. After Quotient devastated the population of Portland on September 24, the home had become the unofficial headquarters of Ops' recovery efforts.

Ashley sipped her Coors light. "Yeah, but they're probably stars of delusion based on the polls."

Searly nodded and said ruefully. "Yeah."

Now thirty-one, Searly was a rarity in that she was a true redhead with blue eyes. Her short hair was in a bob cut. Like all true redheads, she had lots of freckles covering her pretty but very pale skin. Searly was petite and had a square-shaped head that was oddly attractive. Her breasts were small, but so was her bottom, to her a winning a trade-off. Searly tended to dress like she was in fifth grade, lots of printed T-shirts, bright colors, and gym shoes. Tonight she wore pink pants and a white sweat shirt with a picture of Bugs Bunny printed on it.

John Bogut, known by most in Ops as Thunder, came to the door, holding, ironically, a Victory Beer. The fifty-three-year-old Ops veteran who was born in Philadelphia but moved to Australia as a child, Thunder had a chiseled, weathered face with gray hair, blue eyes, and a pointed gray beard. He was a sturdy man, probably six-two and in the 220 range. He was wearing a white collared shirt and olive-green pants, no shoes or socks.

"Crickey, sheilas, you should come on in. INN is calling it for Strong."

Ashley looked at Searly. "It's been a long month. I had hoped something would happen."

"Yeah, me too."

Sullenly, they rose and came inside like teenagers forced to obey curfew by strict parents. Inside, the living room was bright compared to outside, which was lit just by the moon and the single porch light. A cozy if slightly dated room, it was mostly brown and white with a lot of pictures on the wall. The main furnishings were two sectionals pushed together to face a wall television and a slew of paintings of Mount Saint Helens, all created by Ashley's mother.

Thunder sat in the green lazy-boy recliner. Ashley sat on the white sofa, while Searly pulled up a chair from a desk that sat under the front window. Searly drew the maple curtains and turned on more lights.

On INN, a woman wearing more make-up than a clown stated, "And it is over. INN is declaring Shy Strong the winner."

"They outghtta know. They probably have demons in Hell helping her," muttered Searly.

Thunder chuckled. "Possibly."

Searly felt a text. She said to the others, "It's mom. She wants to know if we can move to Canada."

"Won't matter if the Consortium gets their way. It is all the same to them," said Thunder grimly.

"Yeah. It sucks."

Searly then sent texts to Chase in Europe, Tripper in Mississippi, a response to her mom, a text to the Kents, and a final text to Mark Meachum, which she knew he would forward to Sam Grant.

Then she leaned back. "What do we do now?"

Ashley said, "There's nothing we can do. We had our shot at stopping them six weeks ago and we blew it. We just have to keep helping the people still alive around Portland and hope the others come up with something."

"I guess so," said Searly sadly.

On September 24, the inner cabal of the Consortium, led by Calico Kelkirk, energized the alien Quotient to absorb the lives and souls of the majority of people in the Portland metro area. Quotient then took thousands of people from around the world to Mars, including the Consortium members that were part of the ritual.

Nearly two million people in Portland not only died but lost their souls.

Searly, Thunder, Ashley, and Tripper O'Sullivan had gotten to Portland, but they were too late. They would have died as well, but Tripper realized at the last second that the earth might protect them, and they sought cover in the sewers.

During the intervening six weeks, Ashley, Thunder, and Searly had been working hard in the Portland area to help the survivors. Exhausted and distraught, Tripper had returned to his office in Tupelo to recover. Because Ashley was from Centralia, which was just ninety miles north of Portland, her home had become the sort of unofficial headquarters of the trio.

The work was devastating for the team. They had to look at their failure every day. The fact that they had just been too late wasn't relevant. They all felt tremendous guilt . . . and tremendous anger.

Ashley's father, Ron, was a tall man with gray hair, a big nose, and glasses. He looked like an accountant, but he was actually a school district administrator. Now 53, he was in reasonably good shape, for he and his wife, Eve, walked a mile three times a week. Eve, 52, was a customer service manager for a commercial lines insurance brokerage. They were both mostly working and waiting for retirement.

They had purchased the home when they married in 1990, and it was long paid for. They had an RV, but rarely used it. They had become homebodies.

To facilitate Ops' operations, Ron and Eve had basically retreated to the west side of the house to stay out of the way. Ashley's old room was still there, for she visited often — well, other than the months she spent with Thunder in Mars prison before their escape — and slept over at times.

Tonight, the McMillians were in their bedroom, already asleep.

Searly received a text. She was startled, because it was from Dr. Vanessa Morgan of Special Ops. In September, they had discovered Searly's inner chest had burn scar tissue. Ops was working on analyzing this.

SEARLY, I HAVE NEWS. CAN YOU CALL ME TOMORROW AT 9?

Her fingers shaking, she responded.

SURE DOC!

Then she put the phone down and fell very quiet.

Searly had joined Ops in 2007 when Searly's best friend, Kathie Vasquez, was possessed and her soul ultimately destroyed by Quafara, the first torture magician who resurrected herself from Hell by using Kathie's body. A few months later, Quafara attacked Searly and her new paranormal friend, Carlie. Carlie was killed during that battle, while Searly suffered a stroke. Most elemental channelers could use telekinesis to control the four ancient Greek 'elements' of earth, air, wind, and fire. The stroke left her able to channel only fire.

That hadn't handicapped her. She became one of Ops best agents. She had met her husband, Clarke Kent, through Ops in 2009, and he had been killed in the battle to save the undersea kingdom of Atlantia from Quafara and her lover, Elkrod, in 2015.

But just before the Portland attack, she'd discovered something odd in her chest cavity. Scar tissue. There was no explanation. Dr. Morgan had been researching it. It wasn't impairing Searly . . . but it worried her.

Ashley noticed Searly's sudden silence, which was quite outside her normal personality, and asked gently, "Hey, is everything okay? I mean other than the Consortium getting what they wanted with the vapid bitch up there." She pointed at Strong, preparing a speech at a podium.

"Yeah, yeah. Just Chase. Having a hard time," lied Searly.

Ashley knew it was a lie, but she didn't press.

Thunder rose and said, "It's time for one more tinny and bed. My stomach can handle a lot, but not that ratbag's acceptance speech."

"It's a blowout, isn't it?" Joy Delaney asked her boyfriend, Director of Special Operations, Little Jack McGrath, as they sat in his office at the Vegas headquarters of Special Operations watching the returns. A while back, the office had been redecorated in a strange fashion. Now it looked like, according to Joy, the inside of a wristwatch. There were gears for wallpaper and on the marble floor and randomly placed clocks everywhere. The rest of it looked like a set from Office Depot.

"Pretty much," he said with what was for him unusual curtness.

Joy remained silent, worried about Little Jack. Joy Delaney had the ability to control people's actions with visual contact, a skill she had manifested while having an affair with her boss in 2017. While very pretty, twenty-seven-year-old Joy wasn't gorgeous. She had a nice round bottom, nice breasts, good legs, and a happy face. Her hair tended to be straight and parted in the middle, and although a natural blonde she often dyed it lighter. Her eyes were a dull blue, her face pretty, but her nose a little big. Joy was the type of girl that looked good in nice clothes and make-up, looked average without them, and basically was pretty enough that she could get by if she was willing to play to her assets.

Joy had always been the other woman, and at the time of her manifestation had been having an affair with her boss, a defense contractor in Chicago. Her father had left her at a young age, and her mother lived with her aunt due to early onset Alzheimer's.

Joy had experienced difficultly adjusting to Ops. She had always been a very average person . . . but her ability had suddenly made her very atypical. At first, she had floundered. But she had found a mentor and a father-figure in Little Jack, while he found in her a replacement for his late sisters. Frankly, it had started as just recreational sex on the surface, but they both had deep wounds they sought to heal in each other. So far, it had worked.

At the moment, she was sitting on the sofa across from his desk, wearing a pair of light purple pants, a white shirt, and a yellow windbreaker. She had a cup of coffee getting cold on the desk.

"I guess . . . we lost, huh?" asked Joy.

"We lost when Sam and his team couldn't stop her in Dallas in August," he said with unusual moroseness. Normally, he was a charismatic young man who enhanced that with exceptional politeness and people skills. He got things done, but not in a dictatorial fashion. No, he did it the *right* way.

Now thirty years old, he had just a hint of a wrinkle around his eyes, but otherwise looked abnormally young. At six-feet and two inches tall, he had presence but wasn't overtly big. He sported short blonde hair and usually a huge grin. Despite very big ears, he was attractive. His green eyes made him look like a cat.

He dressed very casually and in a very standardized fashion. In public, he almost always wore the same outfit: old jeans, white tennis shoes, a black dress shirt with white vertical stripes, no tie, and always the top button unfastened. He wore the same outfit the way Superman wore the same crime-fighting costume.

Little Jack and his late sister, Sherry, grew up together. They were born to Big Jack McGrath and his first wife, Danielle. Little Jack came in 1990, Sherry in 1991. Big Jack McGrath was a legend in both business and the TM business, but a serious back injury in '85 forced him to retire to the purely fiscal end of the TM business. A wizard with real estate and mining, he was worth several billion dollars. Danielle was his acolyte before she became his wife, and she died in a battle with the Head in late 1991, just months after giving birth to Sherry.

Lisa was his half-sister, and they didn't meet until she was fifteen, but he always accepted her as a full sister, showing the hospitality and family loyalty his father had engrained in him. Little Jack learned everything about TM and business from his father. He idolized him, and when his father died in 2012 from brain cancer, Little Jack came to realize it was up to him to carry on the family name.

As for Lisa and Sherry, well, they were incestuous, but everyone had flaws. The one drawback to being incredibly rich, incredibly invested in torture magic, and incredibly powerful was isolation. They had no peers and had turned to each other in a very intimate manner.

But Little Jack's obsession for the perfect deal and his interest in TM led him to conspire with the late Gary Hart, founder of the International News Network (INN), Dr. Robert Kosar, and serial killer TM Marc Bundy to attempt to open a portal to restore the first torture magicians, Elkrod and Quafara, to Earth and under their control.

The result was catastrophic. All six conspirators died when Ops broke up the attempt to open the portal. Little Jack was infused with a dramatic mix of tachyons, portal energy, and physic heat. Driven insane, he instinctively portaled and was found wandering aimlessly in Detroit a few days later by Ops.

Ops director, Sylvester Starnes, drew the power out of Little Jack, restoring him to normalcy. But Little Jack's time had dramatically changed him. He had seen his destiny if he did not change his ways, and also saw he was the sole hope of redemption for his sisters, now stuck in Hell. As a result, he changed his ways. His sincerity was confirmed by a mental scan by telepath Mary Richardson. Then he took over Ops.

"They tried," said Joy pensively.

"Yeah, trying only counts for kids," he said grimly. And he looked grim, his hands balled in fists as he sent texts in between watching the six screens on the wall to his left, Joy's right.

Then he laughed.

"What is it?" Joy asked, smiling, pleased to see something lighten his mood."

"I gotta give it to Dayne or Strong or whatever she calls herself and the Consortium. This is the sort of plan when I was a TM I'd come up with and try to execute. She did a fine fucking job of shoving it up our ass."

"Oh," said Joy, not sure she understood the humor but not really caring either. She just was glad to see a smile.

But it faded quickly. On the main screen, which had five smaller screens around it, was INN, the International News network, the screens showing the broadcast from different countries. Their lead reporter was a woman with curly black hair wearing a gray suit jacket. She said, "Strong has won more than 35 states and by more than ten points, surpassing even the best projections of recent days."

Little Jack nodded and glanced at his phone. It was 9:15, and basically, it was already over. "At least we'll get to bed early tonight."

"We can fool around."

He shook his head. "Not tonight. I . . . have too much to process. I'm still under enormous pressure to somehow get to Mars and stop Calico. Everyone is into this after her crazy public address — NSA, WSA, CIA, CSIS, MI6, and a bunch of other organizations that don't have acronyms. Everyone wants a piece of her . . . except the Germans. I think they see her as a resource and are keeping a low profile."

"I know. I've heard the phone calls. Some of the people that call and yell at you are quite loud."

"Sorry." She rose. "You're sure you don't want some time to yourself?"

"I'm sure. I gotta figure out what Dayne being in charge means for this mess. I'm sorry."

"Oh."

Distracted and worried, he did not catch her disappointment.

"President Strong . . . it will take getting used to," he muttered.

"I accepted this would happen after Sam lost, and frankly we have more critical issues to handle," said Geneva. From the server room she and Golden Bear had built in the cavern in Siberia, she was on via Op' secure vide app with her younger sister, Medina, who sat with their mother, Geraldine, and the parallel world Colin Ridgeway in the old historical lighthouse home of Geneva's late grandparents. Geraldine now cared for it.

"I agree with you there," said Medina.

They were having a late snack of cinnamon rolls that Geraldine had made earlier in the day.

Now thirty, Medina was a pretty and charismatic young woman. Medina was a pretty and charismatic woman — all Kanes were charismatic — albeit very different from Geneva. She was a little chunky around the waist, but generally hid that with fashionable clothes. Her blonde hair was now very curly, a marked change from her younger days when she kept it straight and long, but it was parted in the middle and flat on top, held back with hairpins. She had wide, bright blue eyes, and always wore a lot of mascara and make-up. Her blush was light pink, and her preferred lipstick was bright red.

Medina and Colin had flown in a few days ago, taking a break from their work in Europe. At the moment, Medina was not wearing any make-up and looked tired. She wore royal blue yoga pants and a very long white sweater with a picture of a black cat on it.

In Russia, Geneva wore gray leggings and a dark blue, bulky sweater with white socks.

Now fifty-three, the Colin Ridgeway of the parallel dimension looked younger, showing few of the wrinkles and sagging typical of men his age. He had curly brown hair that looked like a wig but wasn't, sharp blue eyes, and a curt and almost manic manner. He was overweight by about forty pounds but hid it well.

The parallel Colin and the native Colin were similar in their backgrounds, at least until around 2004 when Zenith began moving back and forth frequently between the dimensions, diluting the parallelism. Colin had been a barrister but turned to the stage. On June 10, 1998, a Wednesday, while he was the lead in Hamlet in London, his younger sister, Nicola, did not show. After the show ended, Colin raced to her flat to find she had vanished. That led him into the world of the paranormal, where he found she had been kidnapped by a TM named Whitaker. Colin dispatched him, but Nicola died. Afterwards, he joined MI6.

Colin wasn't paranormal or a channeler, but he had enough latent channeling ability that he could use totems, which were objects that bestowed moderate paranormal abilities on the holder. A totem holder wasn't going to move a building. They might be able to move the balls on a pool table.

The native Colin Ridgeway had been killed several years ago by the TM Necra. The parallel Colin had come to Geneva's world, our world, to aid the team in stopping some fundamental danger Radar had seen — Radar was Jared patience, the late Meredith Patience's uncle, who had been trapped more than a decade earlier by Zenith in the parallel dimension. Radar was a seer, and since being attacked and "killed" by the Four Cornered Wheel in the body of Julie Julian, he'd been hiding undercover in Europe, where he remained on this night.

Colin was wearing yellow pants with black pinstripes and a yellow T-shirt. He was devouring the rolls.

Joining them at the kitchen table was Geraldine, once an Ops agent and now just a mom. She looked like an older version of Genera, with mostly gray hair now. She wore flannel pajamas with pictures of black cats. The television in the kitchen was on, but the rest of the lighthouse was silent and dark. Outside, it was raining lightly and turning very cold, some snow flurries mixed in with the rain already.

INN was broadcasting yet another live interview of the winner of the election, Shy Strong. Now thirty-six, Strong — who was really a powerful channeler allied with the Consortium named Amy Dayne — smiled a charming, winning smile of white teeth, red lips, and blue eyes. She had long, slightly curly auburn hair and it flipped back as she turned. Petite, she was glowing with victory and looked politely sexy in a red and black checkered skirt, white hose, and a white blouse. A jacket matching the skirt was worn unbuttoned as she stood before the female reporter.

"You feel pleased?" asked the reporter, dark-haired Osa Carerra, the throng behind her chanting and waving victory signs.

She smiled glowingly. "Of course! I'm mostly happy for my supporters, though, the people that want this country to return to a land of freedom and justice for all — a land of fairness and equality."

The crowd cheered.

Osa asked, "Many people are alarmed by the actions of the woman identified as Calico Kelkirk, who seems to be behind thousands of random disappearances . . . who may be quite made given her statement that she's on Mars. How will you deal with that?"

"Like I deal with every problem, talking it out and getting fats, then coming to a resolution. That's the way a woman and a *real* President deals with problems," she said, making a not-so-subtle swipe at Trump.

The crowd cheered.

"She is quite magnetic, isn't she?" said Colin to no one in particular.

Geneva sighed and rolled her eyes. "Oh, spare me. You just like her looks."

Medina laughed. Colin said, "My dear Miss Kane, that is simply not so. Granted, she is quite easy on the eyes . . . but that's not it." He shook his head as he watched the screen. "No, she truly has it, the infinite, impossible, indefinable 'it' that makes the charismatic truly charismatic."

Medina retrieved the orange juice from the refrigerator and as she poured a glass said, "You're just a windbag. You have a crush on her. Maybe you should text her for a date. She is a widow. Allegedly."

Colin chuckled. "Don't dare me, dear Medina. I'll take you up on it. And under my seductive charms, she would give away all of her secrets."

He laughed and Geneva rolled her eyes.

"She *is* extremely charismatic," said Medina thoughtfully.

In a tone was awed and very quiet, Geneva said, "Good Lord . . . that could be it."

"What did you say?" asked Geraldine.

Looking stunned, Geneva looked at her mother, then quickly at her sister and then fixed her gaze on Colin. "You said it, Colin. She's *magnetic.*"

"An apropos use of the term, surely?"

Geneva ignored him. Medina was about to speak again, but Colin waved a hand to indicate to drop it, and Medina did. That was a rarity. Medina usually didn't listen to anyone. But she really liked Colin, and they had forged a bond during their adventures in Europe in recent months.

Geneva finally looked at her mother, then her sister, then Colin. Then she said, "We know TMs and channelers are not identical. Most are like us Kanes, elemental channelers. There's also torture magicians. But there are variants, those that can channel a basic force. Marrina was the best example of that. She could channel gravity."

Geneva paused, recognizing that her mom and Colin had instantly picked up her train of thought. Medina hadn't and was shifting in her chair uncomfortably.

To connect the dots for her younger sister, Geneva said, "Suppose Strong can channel *magnetism.* That could affect the aura. That could affect not only her aura but the aura of those around her . . . possibly even transmit via television signals."

"That last bit is a tad of a stretch," said Colin, "but you may well be onto something with the start. Magnetism does impact the aura.

She could make herself very charismatic and then carry the rest through simple good interviews."

"She's conned the world," said Geraldine softly.

Geneva chuckled. "Well, only a bit. I mean, you don't need much to beat Trump. Outside his base, he's as unpopular as the IRS."

"How do we prove such a thing?" asked Colin, now clearly thoughtful, rubbing his chin and sitting up straight.

"Difficult," said Geneva. "And it's just a theory. She could have some type of completely different power. Anyhow, I'll email Sylvester and Little Jack. They'll have to look into it. We have other things to do."

Geraldine said, "You mentioned the Middle East?"

Geneva nodded. "We've got to find out anything we can about what we've learned here in Siberia. We have the sword. Golden Bear can remain in Siberia and monitor the complex. The three of us need to find someone that can help us analyze it, and Sylvester got us a contact. Ops knows nothing of it, and the same scans they do in Vegas on it can be done in Cairo. That's where we're going tomorrow. I'll meet you in Cairo."

There were cheers from the television as Strong raised her hand. She smiled a truly gloating smile and raised her hands to cheers from the crowd.

Finally, Colin said morosely, "Too bad that assassination attempt failed."

Geneva nodded and said, "All we can hope is that once she's officially in office she starts making moves that expose her motives. Sometimes that happens. Sometimes there's unintended consequences in the plans of the paranormal."

Chapter Three
Wake Up!
November 3 and 4, 2020

The unintended consequences, of course, were what *no one* knew.

And there would be consequences of Amy Dayne, a.k.a. Shy Strong, winning the election. For Amy Dayne, unknown to everyone, was one of the most powerful channelers in the world. She was one of the Quartet, a group of paranormals that had been created through experimentation starting in the 1970s by the Consortium scientist Sigurdsson. They were all very powerful and in ways even he couldn't fully appreciate.

Part of that was she was strongly pulling on the probability cloud particles dissipated throughout the world, including Southern California. That had been a PC hotspot since Jennifer Saunders became a 'soul' survivor when Insectia went on her rampage and killed everyone but Saunders in the Arizona complex in 2004.

Even Dayne herself did not fully understand this, nor did Sigurdsson, her mentor.

The impact of Dayne pulling so dramatically on probability had a recursive effect on many of those with probability cloud influence.

One such person was Jennifer Saunders, in a coma ever since her battle with Quotient on Storm Island back in May.[2] Since that time,

---

[2] See TM 3.4 "The Island the World Forgot"

she had lay in a bed in the Ops trauma hospital wing in Vegas, her room endlessly beeping the same hypnotic tone that meant nothing was happening over and over and over . . . and over.

Until Trump stepped to the podium and admitted defeat.

At that moment, Jennifer Saunders woke up.

"Oh, my God," said nurse Martha Cartwright as she entered Jennifer's room. Martha was an older woman with gray hair and glasses, the type that looked like she ruled the ward with an iron fist.

"Uh . . . hi. Could I get some clothes?" asked Jen. Her unruly brown hair was laying across her shoulders, some gray showing now. Her blue eyes were bright, but her face was very pale. She looked extremely thin. In March, she had been sixty pounds overweight. After being knocked into a tachyonic coma by Quotient's attack in May, she had been in Ops' Vegas complex in the ICU room. Months of IV feeding had left her underweight for the first time since early childhood.

Martha said, "Of course. Let me get Doctor Morgan.".

Anissa said internally to Jen, "Boy, we sure stained her undies!"

"Stop that. Where are we? What's going on?' asked Jen.

Oscar quickly answered, "This is an Ops ward."

Jen slowly sat up. "I'm stiff."

"Good grief! Look at the calendar," said Oscar.

On the far wall was a calendar with a picture of a dog kissing a cat. It was crossed off to the current date, which of course was November 3.

"Oh, Lord," said Jen. "Can our life get any stranger?"

Once upon a time, there was a woman named Jennifer Saunders who lived a quiet, sheltered life as a scientist. But   Jennifer was *not* a fairy tale princess. Her entire life was defined by loss.

Jennifer was a pretty woman, though oblivious to this fact. In 1999, she joined Special Operations, the government organization that studied the paranormal. Jen was only twenty-two years old and fresh out of Stanford. At that time, she had unruly brunette hair that ran in waves past her shoulders, pretty blue eyes, and nice but chunky figure. Generally, she dress was . . . dowdy. But to Jen, her appearance was unimportant. Her life was her work.

Jennifer had never been gregarious. Her mother had died in a car accident when she was only five, and her father had just died a couple of months before she joined Ops, so she was alone. Once at Ops, she stepped in to carry on his work related to attempting to clone a human with a soul. They were also studying Subject Six, the alien creature in a coma ever since the crash landing in '87.

The complex where Jennifer worked was buried underground in the remote Arizona desert. Jennifer liked this environment. She was focused on her work. Jen *enjoyed* the work. She loved science. It had rules and limits, no *emotion*.

Emotions terrified Jennifer Saunders. When only seven years old, she had witnessed her best friend, June, murdered and dismembered by June's mother. The result was that Jen had developed dissociative identity disorder, creating seven alters that functioned on a subconscious level to protect Jennifer from the trauma. When joining Ops, she only knew of one alter: Patty, her little girl self.

Jen had also been molested by her uncle. He later attacked Jen and her roommate, Karen, in their dorm in Stanford. Karen later killed herself, traumatized by the attack. Uncle Bill had terminal cancer and died shortly after as well.

Suffice it to say, Jennifer did not trust people.

She trusted science.

In Arizona, she was successful in her enterprise. Robby was born, a clone with a soul, verified by an out of body experience during a medical emergency.

On April 16, 2004, Subject Six, nicknamed Insectia by one of the staff, woke up. She wasn't happy about having her DNA tampered with, having her soul damaged. She killed the forty-plus members of the compound, including Robby, and including Jennifer and her best friends and co-workers, Shauna Thompson and Allan Elliott. But Jennifer's DID protected her. Insectia was a bee-like creature, although technically more related to the order of hymenoptera, the wasp. Mentally, she was part of a collective consciousness with advanced telekinetic and telepathic abilities. Her telepathic attacks were blunted by Jen's unique DID framework. Jen survived.

So did Allan. He clandestinely had been working for the Consortium, a band of paranormals, businessmen and politicians that supposedly were out to protect the world from global warming. However, Allan had secretly bonded with Insectia, betraying the team.

Later, they found out Zenith, Oscar Clegg's torture magician ex-wife, had actually awakened Insectia in an attempt to ensure Jen would die and not threaten her plans. Torture magicians were the most dangerous of paranormals, ones that used the pain and adrenaline generated through torture to power telekinesis and other skills.

Two others survived the attack in the complex, although 'survive' was a relative term. Oscar Clegg, Jen's 78-year-old mentor who had a bald head and scruffy gray beard; and Anissa Radovich, a young nurse with chipmunk cheeks, curly blonde hair, and a buxom frame. Each had their souls somehow grafted to Jennifer's psyche. Their bodies were dead. Their souls were not.

Jen was now a 'soul' survivor, a very rare paranormal event. With Jen, Oscar and Anissa formed a team that stopped Insectia from breeding a new colony in the hills outside San Diego.

During the final battle, Insectia inadvertently infused Jen's friends Brent and Sheila with telekinetic powers. Jen also had a shard of Insectia's psyche fused to her mind, as Oscar and Anissa had been. Insectia was really named Jaye, the closest translation in our language, something Jen learned later.

Allan was captured. He had been in Special Operations prison since that event . . . for the most part.

About a year after the attack, Jen was working for General Emerald Jon Jameson and Special Operations. Jameson and Clegg had been friends for more than thirty years. Jen's mission was to protect a research project in Oklahoma. Unknown to anyone, it had already been secretly taken over by Zenith.

Using a gem that transferred the user between dimensions, although not space, Zenith displaced Jen into the nearest parallel world, a world where Zenith's plans succeeded. There, the parallel Shauna was murdered, and Jen went into a catatonic coma.

For a year, Anissa took over Jen's body and fought with the resistance in the parallel world. But they were losing. Badly. During this time, Clegg, trapped in Jen's psyche, completed a complex integration of Jen and her seven personalities: Patty was really a young, child version of Jen. They integrated with the system that included: Liza, a spiky-haired, nose-ring wearing teen who kept order; Prisoner, a girl locked in an asylum with no mouth so she wouldn't give away the secret of Uncle Bill's violations, a secret Jen had subconsciously repressed; Cara, a blonde young girl who held Jen's anger; Don, the sullen teen with messy hair who played basketball by himself; Honey, a very young girl; and Rudolph, a very young boy. They also integrated the aspect of Jaye's personality.

They returned to our world to escape a devastating combat loss in the parallel world in 2006 but had to return immediately.

Fully whole for the first time in her life, Jen spent the next four years fighting losing battles in the parallel world. Movement across worlds grew more complex as they grew more divergent. Jen changed, maturing form a scared young woman to a bold fighter.

Seeing defeat as inevitable in the parallel world, seeing millions killed and enslaved, Jen needed another plan. Jaye suggested calling her people, and in 2010 Jen returned to her and our world to call them, planning to then portal them into the parallel world — the ultimate surprise attack. But wary of Jennifer, Tripper O'Sullivan foiled that plan.

Jen returned to the parallel dimension a failure.

In 2014, Jen returned knowing from the parallel world and other sources that Zenith on our world was close to instigating another successful drilling project, one that would give her access to Soloman's Liquid and allow her plans of conquest to continue. Zenith was obsessed with security, traumatized by being held as a child in the concentration camps of the Nazis during World War II.

Soloman's Liquid imbued female TMs with immortality and changed males into crazed werewolf-like creatures, an unstoppable if short-lived army. It had obvious benefits for Zenith.

Jen helped Ops halt that project. Zenith was arrested and incarcerated in Atlantia, a hidden kingdom under the arctic ice, by its exceptional queen, Marrina.

Jen then realized she had a way to stop the parallel Zenith.

Which she did. With the aid of the parallel Joshua Clegg, Oscar's son, she saved the parallel dimension and together they rewrote it. But this action made it much less parallel to her native and our present Earth, which made moving back and forth more or less impossible.

However, Meredith Patience breached the parallel dimensional barrier in desperation in 2018 to escape a TM named Everett. Meredith lay in a coma for roughly two years, but once she woke up and Saunders' and the parallel Ops team realized the potential dangerous on our native Earth, they sought return. Shortly afterwards, Geneva escaped from the Martian prison where Calico had placed her by somehow breaching to the parallel world. Together, they were able to return to Jen's, our, native world.

That had led to the battle with Ops and Calico's consortium team, aided by Quotient, on Storm Island. That resulted in Meredith's death and Jen's coma.

And now she was awake. Two people arrived with the nurse, Doctor Morgan and Sylvester Starnes.

Dr. Morgan was currently the lead Ops doctor at the trauma center. Ops agents were her purview. She was a tall woman with a flat face, long brownish-blonde hair, and green eyes. Now thirty-six, she had graduated from the University of Miami and rotated to Ops three years earlier based on some superb work in the trauma centers of Florida. Her face was already wrinkled, the legacy of enjoying the sun. She had obviously dressed in a hurry, wearing black slacks and a white shirt with a white physician's coat over it, her hair an unruly mess and her face lacking any make-up.

Sylvester Starnes was the current head of Special Operations, having replaced General Jameson in 2014. Sylvester had a very handsome, chiseled face, dark brown eyes, and gray hair, the sort of man that defined distinguished. At six-foot three and 225, he was also well-built physically. His body was covered in scars, a legacy of being immortal but not invulnerable.

In 1776 at the age of twenty-three, the TM Sylvester Starnes made a mistake and was caught by a witch named Deliah. She cursed him, made him immortal and removed his ability to channel TM. Since then, he had largely wandered, only occasionally taking an interest in human affairs — until 2014, when he had taken over Special Operations when General Jameson was fired.

Few trusted him his first years as director. Part of that was the abrupt departure of Jameson, who was beloved. Most of it was Sam Grant, the leader of field ops at the time, thought Sylvester was a dog on a leash, and that if the leash were removed, he'd be a biter, so to speak. But Sylvester had proved his attempts to change were grounded in who he was as a man, not the curse, when he fought off Everett in his attempt to save Meredith Patience.

Once Sam left a couple of years ago, Sylvester had been the one to put Little Jack in charge, and the operations now ran smoothly without the undercurrent of tensions that had marked the Grant-Starnes regime.

"By Struth! Jennifer! You *are* awake!" he said, making it clear he had doubted the alarm. He was wearing a brown sweater and black pants, looking like he had thrown on whatever was handy to get dressed.

He moved to hug her, but Doctor Morgan brushed him back to do some checks. Then she looked at Sylvester, "She seems fine. Disturbingly so."

"What, pray tell, does that mean?" he asked.

"She's pretty much ready to go. Her metabolism is off the charts." She paused and added, "This was an atypical coma, a tachyonic influx or something, right?"

"True."

"That might be something to do with it. She's free to move about but keep her nearby in case something happens while I do some deeper lab work and such. Deal?"

"Of course," said Sylvester.

Annoyed, Jen said, "I'm fine! Look, Sylvester, we must talk! I remember important things! Is Quotient still lose? Is everyone okay?"

"Indeed, we shall talk, for Quotient still is lose and the situation is most grave." He turned to the nurse. "Get this woman ready and in my office in fifteen minutes!"

Twenty-five minutes later, Jen was wearing borrowed jeans that had tears in the knees and were a bit loose on her, a white blouse with red roses that buttoned down the middle, and brown flats. She sat in a chair in Little Jack's office.

With her were Little Jack, wearing his typical pinstriped shirt and slacks; Joy, wearing a lavender skirt and sleeveless top with a white sweater; Sylvester, wearing the same clothes; and Sly Silverstone, wearing a green hairband, a green and yellow swirling colored blouse, black skirt, black hose, and black shoes.

In March of 2020, Sly Silverstone was a stunningly beautiful eighteen-year-old senior who attended an illustrious parochial high school in upscale Long Island. She was gorgeous, rich, well-liked, and intelligent. She had short, straight blonde hair that curled at the ends. It was a nice mix of short and long. Her front bangs were long. Her eyes were sky blue, and her lips pouting and pretty. Her face was perfect, her figure was perfect, she was perfect. She was the sort of girl that appeared on posters used by colleges for advertising.

But her mobster father found she was working with federal officials to take him down, for she had discovered he had ordered a hit on Sly's mother. That led to her being buried alive and her discovery of her channeling ability. After killing with her father, she'd been brought to Ops and joined.

Remotely, Little Jack had an Ops version of Skype connection going on a huge screen that was behind a whiteboard he had rolled back on the right wall of the office, usually behind the main door when it was open. Golden Bear was on remote from Siberia. Geneva, Medina, and Colin were all on private military flights arranged by Sylvester to get them to Cairo, albeit from two entirely different starting points. They all wore jeans and hoodies, dressed for travel. Geraldine was on remotely from the lighthouse kitchen, the rolls now long devoured by Colin. She was wearing a flower-print dress under a blue sweater.

Searly, Thunder, and Ashley were connected from the living room in the McMillian home in Centralia. They hadn't gone to bed yet. Thunder looked a little drunk. Searly wore a bright red blouse and black shorts. Ashley wore jeans and a purple sweatshirt. Thunder wore jeans and a white T-shirt under a black leather jacket.

Finally, they had one of the humanoid Radar robots from a hideout in Berlin that looked like a cheap motel. He wore jeans and a black T-shirt with a print of Elvis Presley.

Radar was known to Ops as the late Meredith Patience's uncle, John Patience. He was tall, well over six feet, and gaunt with curly gray hair, a very weathered face, a thick mustache, and haunted blue eyes. Probably in his early fifties, but in good shape . . . well, of course, were he human he would've been in good shape.

After the TM Zenith wiped out Meredith's family, Radar went after her, but that got him portaled into Jen's parallel dimension, where he got his ass-kicked and wound up surviving only by being rescued and having his body shoved into a gold, oddly shaped robot that looked like a cross between a vacuum cleaner and an Oldsmobile. But he'd since created several humanoid robots since his return to this, his native Earth. Those looked like a typical man in his fifties with curly, grayish hair and a good physique.

"Where is everyone else?" asked Jen.

"Sam got framed and is in deep trouble, so he's gone deep undercover with the aid of the Neutrals and Jameson. I just don't have time to set up the secure channels and loop them in. I'll fill them in later. And Tripper didn't answer his phone, but he's probably asleep. The guy never answers after midnight. Everyone else is, well, working," said Little Jack. He sat behind the desk, Joy sitting in a guest chair to his right. Sly sat on the sofa nearby, while Sylvester stood behind Jen, arms folded over his chest.

"Okay," said Jen. "Where do we start?"

"What's the last thing *you* remember?" asked Sylvester of Jen.

"I . . . the last thing I remember is the battle on the island. I saw Meredith . . . saw her die. Did anyone other than Meredith . . . pass away?"

"No," said Little Jack.

"Thank God."

"I'm glad you're awake," said Geneva, obviously relieved.

"We all are, obviously," added Colin.

"Thanks," said Jen thoughtfully. Then she paused, all eyes on her. Internally, she had a question for Oscar.

"How do I approach what we learned?"

"Just describe it. Once they know what we face, perhaps they'll have some ideas."

"Okay."

Jen took a deep breath and looked at all of them. "Some of you I know well. Some of you I don't know at all." Sly smiled politely. Jen continued and said, "But I think all of you have read enough files to know I have what's called dissociative identity disorder. When Jaye attacked . . . in the complex . . . Oscar and Anissa were stuck in my head. But in addition, I have my own alter personalities in my head. Most of them are children, because the . . . the trauma that happened to me happened when I was a child.

"As a result, I dissociate, disconnect from reality, quite easily. That's where my alters were created, though I've since learned . . . other things," she said. She hesitated, for her life with her alters was still somewhat private, and she didn't want to share the fact that she had learned they were all other people, other souls, who had been put by God to share her body to help her. She wasn't sure everyone would be on board with this knowledge, and it wasn't relevant to the task at hand.

Geneva had known Jen for many years and sensed her conflict, so Geneva gently said, "We understand that concept. You're saying the tachyonic coma Quotient inflicted is related to dissociation?"

Pleased for support, Jen smiled and nodded. "Yes, this coma I fell into after my . . . our . . . battle with Quotient certainly was some type of dissociative event, but *very* different from dissociation due to my disorder, or due to the shock that caused me to go, uhm, catatonic — back in '05 and '06, when Oscar integrated our personalities.

"This event was triggered by *Patty* to protect us. Patty is my child self who . . . witnessed a terrible crime," said Jen, unable to tell so many people in so public a venue her most private and horrible secret. "In many ways, she, not I, is our core personality.

"We understand," said Geneva for more support.

"Thanks. Uh, anyhow . . . when we engaged in battle with Quotient on the island, he attacked us telepathically. Quotient . . . tried to consume us, to convert not just our body but our soul into energy."

"Yes, that's what he does," confirmed Sylvester grimly.

"The alters interpreted this as him trying to remove them, to detach them from us, so they fought. We were able to fight this, because I've been through a battle like this before. My paranormal situation, for lack of a scientific term, was created by the telepathic alien Subject Six . . . Insectia, or Jaye, as we finally wound up calling her. As some of you know, I defeated her because she thought I was a collective consciousness, but I am not. The souls that make up my dissociative identity disorder, plus Anissa and Oscar who merged with me when she destroyed the complex, are unique individuals."

Joy and Sly for the most part looked utterly bewildered. But everyone else was giving Jen intent concentration.

"So when Quotient attacked me, I had a similar defense to use, my *unique* mental structure. Alter personalities are separate soul entities within my body. I share my physical body with other souls. The theology of this is not in debate today. This is how it works . . . what I learned a few years ago."

She took a deep breath. "During the battle, we were fighting on multiple levels. Patty, however, *doesn't* fight. She's a child. She was scared. But somehow, she separated from me during the battle and engaged Quotient . . . on her own."

"By Jove!" shouted Colin.

"That sounds dangerous," added Geneva. "And please ignore Colin's inappropriate outburst. We've yet to find anyone that can teach him manners and tact."

Jen smiled. "It's okay." She took a deep breath, and internally got some support from Anissa and Jen. "The key is how Patty was interacting with him *before* everything fell apart, and I use the word him with precision. Quotient is a male."

She paused.

"And Quotient is a child — perhaps a toddler."

Stunned, no one said anything. Then Little Jack said, "You're certain?"

Jennifer nodded. "It's undoubtable." She paused. "I have no idea where he's from or if his parents are here."

Geneva said, "Quotient was awakened from the ice in 949 and put back into it. We know from Lexx and the other records we've uncovered over the years that aliens have always landed on Earth, usually badly. Most likely, Quotient came here from somewhere else with mommy and daddy a long, long time ago and somehow he got frozen and stayed alive. I don't think there are others. We would have found them by now."

Jen said, "I hope you're right."

"Me, too. Let's deal with Quotient for the moment," said Geneva. "We know he's here. One step at a time."

"Agreed," said Sylvester.

Again, everyone was quiet for a few seconds. Then Radar said, "So can he, uh, like, talk and stuff? Is he, like, two?"

"Patty's impression is he's not a baby, but younger than her. Perhaps four? That's an impression, not a fact."

"That's a wide range," said Geneva. "But even knowing this, how does this help us? He's a male . . . but a male *what*?"

"I'm not sure. Those are good questions, Geneva," said Jen thoughtfully.

Internally, Anissa said, "She's smart. And she has the same questions I do!"

Suddenly, internally Oscar said, "Mary. Mary was attacked and is also in a similar coma. She's a telepath."

Realizing the direction of Oscar's thoughts, Jen externally snapped her fingers and asked Sylvester, "Is Mary still in her coma?"

"Yes," said Sylvester grimly.

"She *didn't* wake up like I did?" asked Jen, relaying the surprise she felt from Oscar internally.

"Nope," said Little Jack.

"Darn," said Jen sullenly. "Oscar is confident we woke up because of a probability cloud event. What happened today?"

Geneva immediately answered, "Shy Strong won the Presidential election."

"Who?" asked Jen.

Little Jack quickly briefed Jen on the background of Strong and Ops' battles to stop her. Then he added with a chuckle, "In fact, the instant Trump conceded, meaning she was officially the winner, you woke up."

Jen nodded. "She has to be using probability cloud influences."

Sylvester said, "She's using power most grand, that is for certain. We tried to stop her in August with utter failure. It is reasonable to assume the PC is part of her powers. But why would that awaken you?"

"Subconsciously, we probably drew on the PC. She probably subconsciously let go once she achieved her goal." Jen sighed. "Oscar's theory is the same would happen to Mary, because she's also PC influenced. But perhaps she is not as strong or more seriously injured."

"You feel like Mary can help?" asked Geneva.

"Oscar does. He thought we could use Mary to link my mind to Quotient's, and I could use Patty to talk to him, convince him to be out friend."

"Well, that's out, but there's another, much more basic problem. We don't know how to find Quotient," said Little Jack. "But he may be on Mars."

"Mars?"

Now Little Jack summarized the events of Mars and the Portland massacre. Jen looked shocked and finally said, "This . . . this is *awful*."

Everyone fell silent. Internally, Oscar said to Jennifer, "It's time to throw out an idea."

"I agree," said Anissa. "These guys look defeated. We gotta rally them with something, even one of Doc's lame ideas."

Oscar sighed.

Jen nodded as she internally agreed, then looked at the group.

"Oscar believes there is a way to find Quotient and in a way that he isn't trying to eat us as soon as he sees us."

"Oh? As Starnes there would say, what, pray tell, would that be?" asked Colin.

"I help Calico with her plan to move humanity to Mars."

"That's the most ludicrous idea I've heard since that simpering fool Chamberlain signed the peace treaty with the Nazis!" shouted Colin, and he banged a wall in the Kane's kitchen. The drywall dented.

Medina snapped at him, "You will be fixing that!"

"Sorry," he said sheepishly.

"Well, okay . . . it's a *possibility*," said Little Jack evenly.

"But practical?" asked Sylvester.

"Your tepid attitude makes me doubt it," said Jen, but with a smile.

Little Jack leaned back and made a pyramid with his hands. Sylvester merely frowned.

Radar said, "Let's let her explain."

Geneva made a rare interruption and said, "Let's say for a minute we agree to let you try and do this, Jen. How is that even possible? You *surely* are not suggesting we let Quotient keep eating cities like Portland, continuing to devour souls, so you must have another plan."

"Yes. Well, it's *Oscar's* plan," she said a little sheepishly. "You see, while I was comatose, he was not. He was stuck in this sort of limbo where my brain is represented by endless corridors and rooms, which represent thoughts. He wandered around in my thoughts and devised this plan, which seems more valid now that Mars is already officially founded."

"Can he talk to us? No offense, but we might lose something in the translation," said Radar.

"Valid point," said Sylvester.

"Yes, he can," said Jen.

Jen concentrated and permitted Oscar to control their physical body. In their early days as a 'soul' survivor, Jen had resisted all such attempts, but sixteen years later, she was fully integrated. For the most part, except under extreme stress, they could switch with conscious effort.

The effect was obvious to the team, which was familiar with her situation and all fair astute observers as well. Suddenly, she shifted to her full height and began moving a lot and pacing, body movements typical of Oscar Clegg, not Jennifer Saunders.

"Thank you, all. It is I, Oscar," said Oscar in Jennifer's body and voice.

Joy whispered to Sly, "Do you follow any of this?"

"Not a bit," admitted Sly with a sheepish face.

"Good. Neither do I!"

Little Jack gave a hand gesture to Joy to shush her. She shut up.

"So, what's the plan, Oscar?" asked Geneva.

Oscar held up one of Jen's fingers. "My plan is based on information we learned in the parallel world. If you recall, not long after Zenith pulled us there, Jen's best friend, Shauna, was murdered in the parallel world as well. Horribly murdered, dropped into a vat of acid. Jen went catatonic. During this time, I was trapped in her mind, which led to my integrating her multiple personalities, as well as those of myself and Anissa, which eventually led to us meeting Miss Kane." He paused and took a breath. "During that time, Anissa ran Jen's body as a member of the parallel world's resistance against the parallel Zenith."

Internally, Anissa said, "Ah, ha! I knew it would come back to this, Doc!"

Oscar hated to be called 'doc,' but he ignored her and continued to the team. "Back in '58, the TM Ozz reported seeing a spaceship in Africa. He did. Provided that ship is still here in Africa, we can use its tachyon well to create a localized tachyonic warp field and basically create a door to Mars. The power variable is significant, but it's nothing that can't be overcome with a few weeks spent implementing adaptive technology. Then there's no need for Quotient and all this killing. We offer Calico the deal to use the well and therefore allow technology to move people. Those that are willing, that is. No more kidnapping any longer. No more deaths."

"Aye, but that ship is there no longer," said Sylvester with a shake of his head. "That ship was captured by Necra and buried under her castle. Sam and Meredith freed it back in 2017, but it was taken to Atlantia and dismantled."

Oscar then looked hard at Sylvester. Jen's body had hands on hips, but the aggressive stance was that of an older man as Oscar-Jen said, "There are others. You know that."

"True enough," admitted Sylvester.

"Actually . . . not all ship gone," said Golden Bear suddenly.

Everyone registered some type of surprise, other than Geneva, as Golden Bear added through a static-laced com-link, "Marrina dismantle much of ship, but some technology still with my people, my new Russian Ops team."

"What pieces?" asked Oscar-Jen.

"I not sure."

Sylvester interjected, "This is not relevant. We can get the technology."

He made it clear he wasn't going to elaborate, so no one pushed him. Instead, Geneva said, "Fine. Let's make that a standard assumption. What then?"

Oscar-Jen looked down, then at the feed showing Geneva's face. "I don't believe Calico wants war, from all the indications we've gotten this year. She wants to save the world, sees herself as a patriot, sees herself as the dutiful daughter carrying on the dreams of her father. She has gone to effort to avoid collateral damage when possible. Anything that risks the plan, no, nor anything needed for Quotient, no. But in all other cases, she has spared people."

"Yes, she had an entire prison on Mars," said Geneva. "Listen, I feel I know her best. I talked extensively with her and Kelkirk when they had me captive in January. Calcio told me much of her story, her childhood, and her main problem is she was raised by a rationalizing, compartmentalizing, ethically challenged TM."

"Kelkirk always was a rationalizer," agreed Oscar.

"Yes. I feel the same as you, Oscar, that she wants her plan to succeed. She's so into it, so wrapped up in herself or her father or both, that she can't see how deviant the means to the ends of this plan is. But she wants it to work, and I think if we could give her a, well, shall we say a more cost-effective process, she *would* listen."

Oscar-Jen nodded. "The key is to get her to listen. I believe I, and I mean myself, Oscar, with that pronoun, can get her to listen. She would be willing to believe that I would be willing to help her based on my history with Ops and her father. Zenith, Kelkirk, and I were in a love triangle for decades. I assume Calico knows all her father knew, which means she probably knows me better than anyone. After all, I was married to Zenith for some time[3], and Zenith was Kelkirk's protégé."

"She'll be suspicious," said Geneva immediately. "She is very shrewd."

"That shouldn't matter," said Oscar-Jen. "You see, my idea is very viable. Frankly, once this disaster is over, we should look into it for other things. But it would take weeks if not months, to arrange the proper configuration of the power. During that time, the key is that if we are working for Calico, Quotient does not automatically register us as a threat. That would buy us a few seconds if we can arrange an aggressive action to take him down, and a few seconds is all we

---

[3] See TM novel 1.1 "Torture Magic"

should need. The mental time is more important to the physical time, and that's variable to the user."

"Okay, but what exactly is the attack plan?" asked Radar with some obvious concern.

"Yes, it would seem a plan without a lever. Quotient is more powerful than any of us, all of us," said Colin, sounding more depressed than a suicidal priest.

"Well, as Little Jack pointed out, first we have to find Quotient. If I'm working with Calico, that can likely be achieved," said Oscar-Jen. "I am certain Patty can talk him down, but either way we must strike from the inside. Now that we know he is a sentient being, we must win him over. We have no way to physically destroy him."

"That may not be true any longer," said Geneva quickly. She relayed what they had learned the last couple of days and added, "So if this works, we could destroy him."

"I think that's a reasonable back-up plan, but we have no guarantees your soldier's sword will work," said Oscar-Jen.

"True."

Sylvester interrupted. "The conclusion is obvious, my friends. Geneva, you and your team must reach Cairo and determine if yours is a viable mode of attack. It will take time for Jen to win Calico's trust anyhow. Meanwhile, we gather up our alien ship parts and prepare to speak to Calico about the viability of our . . . alternative."

Geneva suddenly said, "Radar, you're a seer. I know you can only tell us certain things. Are we on track?"

Everyone went dead silent. That included Radar. After a long pause he said, "I have a slightly different objective . . . something I have to keep relatively mum about. No offense, but if you know too much, you could distort events from the path and complicate or even ruin my efforts. I'm already concerned that an event as big as Portland wasn't on my, ah, radar." He paused before adding, "From what I sense, your objectives and mine are dovetailing. In general, I have to keep in hiding snice the ol' 4CW thinks she roasted me. But . . . Calico knowing I'm alive could actually solve a lot of issues for me.

Also, in my robot body, I can switch out my consciousness before Quotient can zap my ass."

"The aura is not the mind," said Geneva firmly.

"Agreed in normal human terms, but I'm far from that. My aura is tied up with my sentient consciousness, so trust me, I'm right on this."

"Okay, so what do you need?" asked Oscar-Jen, showing a little confusion.

"I keep one of my robot bodies work with you as a bodyguard. I'm perfectly happy informing Calico that I'm multiple robots, which explains why I was picked for the job. Besides, it might not hurt her to know Quotient *isn't* invincible. Anyhow, if what happens is what I generally foresee happening, you'll damn well need me."

"Very well," said Oscar-Jen.

"It's a very risky plan," said Little Jack quickly.

"Nay, 'tis on a sound foundation," countered Sylvester quickly. "The main risk is for Miss Saunders and associates."

"I also worry about doing a deal with the devil and what that will mean for Jen," said Geneva.

"I can handle that," said Oscar-Jen. "I'll be in control most of the time. I'm used to moral dilemmas." He-she chuckled. "As I said, I was married to Zenith. I . . . am not a perfect man. I can handle it."

Oscar had experimented on his fellow prisoners in the concentration camps, something only he, Jen, Anissa, and Jen's alter Cara knew.

"I agree with that," said Geneva. "There's one condition."

"Sure," said Oscar-Jen.

"Neither Calico nor any of her associates gets a pass for their past crimes. We can work with them to bring them down, but when this is over, they are held accountable for their slaughter of the people in Portland, to say nothing of all of their other crimes." She paused. "Does anyone on the call object?"

"I think we should just kill her six ways to Sunday," said Radar.

"Seconded," said Colin

Searly immediately said, "I am *not* being part of an assassination plan!"

Little Jack interrupted. "Calico is going to fight to the end. We probably won't get a choice. But we're not out to kill her. That could turn her into a martyr. And if nothing else, the information she knows about the paranormal and the Consortium makes her invaluable to us. We just want to agree that she is held accountable."

No one objected.

"Good. Then let's go forward. Our first step would be securing the technology. We can't bluff Calico. We need to have her magic fix. Meanwhile, Golden Bear and I can continue our work," said Geneva.

"Fine," said Little Jack.

"Actually, our bigger issue is Mary," said Oscar-Jen. "My original plan to have Patty talk him down was relying on having a telepath to get us inside Quotient's mind. I'm sure Quotient himself is telepathic, but I'd prefer not to have *him* instigate the connection. That might frighten the other alters."

"Well, we have some time. Maybe Mary will wake up," said Little Jack.

"We can't count on that," said Geneva. "But we have time to figure that out."

Colin spoke up. "The other issue is arranging some type of dentate with the wary Calico. Has anyone thought of that? It's not exactly like we can RSVP her to Ops."

"There are ways to get to her," said Little Jack. "That's the *least* of our problems. We just gotta be sure that when Jen talks to her, everything is ready. Once we make that commitment, we lose control. Everything is in Calico's hands."

Thunder said, "Boss, what do we do?"

Little Jack clapped his hands. "Okay, here's the plan, team. Thunder, Searly, Ashley, you continue to help in Portland and push leads there. Joy, Sly and I will continue to research and see if we can find a way to wake up Mary. We also have to deal with our, ah, public enemy friends and see what we can learn on Strong, if she has any weakness, and maybe what putting her in charge of America does for the Consortium. If fucking Tripper ever wakes up, he'll support everyone.

"Kane team, you need to continue to research the sword. Jen, you and Sylvester work with Golden Bear and gather your tech. If necessary, I can spot you Joy and Sly."

"Thanks," said Oscar-Jen.

"Radar . . . what are you doing besides hiding out in a bad motel?" asked Little Jack.

"I've got issues goin' on that are bigger than Dolly Parton's titties. My issues may soon dovetail into yours, but I gotta stay outta this plan. I can't get tied up when I might have to act on what I see for the future."

"A long-winded explanation for doing nothing and eating hotel dinner rolls," joked Colin.

"Hey, don't forget, I'm a robot. There's more than one of me. I'm a lot more capable than you think!"

Chapter Four
Gia DeKnight
November 4, 2020

Anxious and depressed, Searly remained at the McMillian home. She bought some Starbucks and made breakfast, then sat on the porch on the morning of the fourth. At nine, she promptly she called the Ops' on-staff doctor, Doctor Vanessa Morgan. Morgan looked tired, the result of her long night checking on Jennifer Saunders.

Appearing on Skype, Searly noticed that Vanessa looked excited, which Searly hoped meant good news. "Uh, hi, doc."

"Miss McTaggert, thanks for calling. I have an actual update other than telling you I'm working on it. Do you have some time?"

"That's why I'm on the line. I was surprised you called. It's been weeks!" said Searly, which was accurate. She had first seen Doctor Morgan on September 18.

"Well, your case was unique. We really have to thank General Jameson, because he went on a mission to Warsaw and found some rare documents there that broke the key for us. And it's almost all good news."

"Yesssssssssssssss," said Searly with an enormous sigh of relief as she shut her eyes and hit her chest.

"I thought that might relieve you," said Vanessa with a half-smile.

"You're right there, doc! But . . . what's happened to me?"

"Well, it's mostly your situation. Medically, here's what we learned. The scar tissue in your chest, which probably exists in other muscles in your body, is not really scars from burns as we feared. It's a paranormal version of scar tissue."

"From, like, a cut? No one has ever cut my chest — although this psycho TM doctor was going to try once."

"Scar tissue forms from any wound. But this is an effect of paranormal activity via aural channeling. I've discussed this with Jameson extensively, given what he found in Warsaw last week."

"It isn't harmful?"

"Well, we don't know in the long-term, but most likely not. Most likely, the only effect is that, as you get older, you're going to have more issues with being stiff. Need more time in the gym."

Searly made a face. "Ugh. I'd rather it be fatal."

Vanessa laughed. "Oh, stop. Anyhow, when you had the stroke while fighting Quafara in '07, you were left with only the ability to channel fire. That's very rare. It looks like what has happened is that has disrupted the natural aural balance all channelers have. The body can be affected by channeling. Since you have been channeling only fire for thirteen years now, it's disrupted the balance and some of the backflow protection isn't there."

"It won't fail, will it?"

"We don't think so. We measure the ratio at 39%. To give you an idea, Geneva Kane's mother, Geraldine — she was injured long ago in a battle — was at 64% when she was injured and retired, but even then, she had no backflow effects. Her retirement was due to other injuries."

"Wow."

"Yes, wow, indeed! And you're a very active channeler, which might be why you show such effects. I mean, you're always using fire to help against natural disasters, like cleaning up after Hurricane Saturday."

"So . . . what should I do, doc?"

"Continue with life. I have no idea what the long-term effects are, but we'll only learn those by monitoring, and due to the situation with Geraldine Kane and a couple others in history, we seem to be well within the safety margin."

Searly sighed and her relief was obvious and enormous. "That . . . is a load off my mind."

Morgan smiled. "I thought it might be. Look, let's take a little time and set up a plan, but this is going to be fine. I'm here for anything you need."

"Is this all we need?" asked Ashley of Thunder as they shopped in the Centralia target. They were in the cat food aisle, buying cans of tuna and salmon for Ashley's parents two white Persian cats, Fluff and Lint. Ashley wore baggy white shorts and a blue camisole with sandals. Thunder wore jeans and a black shirt that hugged his shoulders and pecs.

Thunder shushed her — he was on his phone. It was roughly mid-day tomorrow in Sydney, where he was calling. Ashley politely waited, studying various cat foods.

Then Thunder said, "Crickey, right, mate." Then he hung up.

"Any luck?" Ashley asked.

"Naw, the ol' doc who helped me in '14 is in rest home now. He was my last contact," said Thunder. He'd called three of his old contacts hoping to find someone that might be able to assist with Mary's coma, but the first two had no suggestions and the last, well, was in a nursing home.

"A pity . . . well, someone will know something."

"I dunno. Ops has been trying for months. Anyhow, doesn't rightly matter now. What was your question?"

"Do we have everything?"

Thunder stared at his phone. "According to this list, yup. No, wait. We need dog treats. I'll go get them."

Ashley waited. Their cart was overflowing, for they were buying for their own needs, Searly, and Ashley's parents — plus a few items to help with their work in Portland. Ashley checked the time. It was 9:43. They were on schedule.

"Hey, is that your dad?"

Ashley turned to see a woman about forty with long, dark brown hair, bangs, blue eyes, and a lot of make-up. Wearing a red blouse with black polka dots, a gold necklace, white pants that hugged her butt, and black shoes, she screamed MILF.

"Uh . . . yeah. His name is John. He's been in Australia for twenty years," said Ashley, curious.

Putting out her hand, she said, "Gia DeKnight. I run a deli down the road. I haven't seen you guys before."

"We're visiting my, uh, grandparents. Relocating up here. I'm Ashley."

"Nice to meet you," she said with a smile. "Is your dad single?"

"As lonely as a tree in the desert," said Ashley, hiding a smirk.

Cocking her head, Gia asked, "You think . . . you mind if I talk to him? He seems interesting."

At that moment, Thunder returned with a box of dog treats. He saw Gia and smiled. "Well, hello."

Gia smiled. "Gia DeKnight. I run Corner Deli."

Ashley moved behind Gia and made a kissing face. Then she said, "We forgot paper towels. I'll be back."

Once she left, Gia moved close to Thunder, her perfume strong. "Your daughter said you've been in Australia. I've never been there, but I plan to go this year. What's it like?"

Thunder studied her. She seemed desperate, but it had been a long time since he'd had any action. His relationship with Ashley was strictly platonic. And he was tired and didn't feel like dealing with the hardship of the suffering. He wasn't a missionary.

"I can tell you more about it. You close by? My, uh, daughter's house is way up yonder."

Gia smiled. "Meet you outside after you check out."

She left, swaying her hips. Ashley quickly returned, having been listening from the other aisle.

"Well, I guess I'm driving home alone," she said with a smirk.

"Yep."

***

Gia's home was a small, middle-class home typical of the area. But it was very neat and well-maintained. The deli was being handled on this day by her staff of three.

They lay in her bed after having sex. Gia said, "That was pretty fun."

"You're a fine Sheila."

"Sheila?"

"Woman, lady."

She smiled. "Thanks. How old are you?"

"Past fifty."

She smiled. "I'm forty. Let me tell you, you're in good shape. You must work out and must have a good job."

He laughed. "I work out a lot, but I dunno about the job thing. I'm in security. That's not always, uh, secure for an old guy like me." He chuckled again. "Forget me. You're a fine one. You have an ex?"

"Yeah, but we parted peacefully five years ago. My daughter is fifteen. She's a non-stop problem, just like I was at that age," she said with a smile. "Don't worry. I just wanted to get laid on my day off, and you're the best-looking guy I've ever seen in that Target."

He chuckled. "Not much completion, is there?"

She smiled. "Nah, not around here. You work security locally?"

"Nah, I'm from Australia. Just here visiting family."

"Yeah, your daughter is cute."

Thunder mentally made a note to give Ashley a swift kick in the ass, then said, "She's a winner, rightly. You want some brekky? I cook a mean omelet."

She smiled. "Sure."

After she put on a brown camisole and jeans shorts over it, he had put on his pants but no shirt and asked, "Ya have a durry?"

"Durry?"

"Ah, cigarette?"

"No, I quit smoking when I got pregnant, sorry."

"It's alright. Let's cook."

Her kitchen was small with furnishings about twenty years old, meaning a lot of orange cabinets and simple white countertops and tile. There were a slew of items on the counter in flower vases, ranging from utensils to actual plastic flowers. The effect was dated but quaint, cute but not forced.

She sat at the small, square, black kitchen table in a black chair the table was covered in math homework and Gia's computer. She asked, "You been here long?"

"Since start of the year," he said, more or less the truth.

"You hear about Portland?"

He winced, but she didn't notice it. "Rightly imagine everyone did. What a bloody nightmare that was."

"Yeah. I had a cousin who lives in Portland, but she was on a business trip in Reno. Lucky."

Thunder concentrated on cooking. Having been one of the few survivors at the epicenter, he really tried to focus on *not* remembering that day. "Yeah. I lost some people."

"I'm sorry about that. I hope they get those people."

"Me, too . . . for everyone's sake."

"You think they're *really* on Mars like that woman on the broadcast said?"

"Don't rightly know. Doesn't matter. I can't do anything about it but try to help the people still here."

She nodded. "I figured you for a tough guy with a good head. I think I was right."

He put the omelet on a plate decorated with roses and said, "You always fall for guys that aren't local?"

"It avoids complications. Life works better that way."

He nodded. "Used to think so . . . after Portland, I know so."

Chapter Five
Fatigue
November 4, 2020

Sam Grant lay on the couch in a cheap living room watching a documentary on the crash of flight PSA 182 in San Diego in 1978. Everyone died when a small plane being flown by a student pilot collided with an airliner.

It fit his mood.

The fifty-one-year-old former Director of Special Operations, Sam Grant was slightly balding, his brown, curly hair fading to gray. He had brown eyes and a short, five-foot and eight-inch wiry frame. He also had a big nose that looked a bit like a vulture's beak. He was in one of many underground rooms in the abandoned California desert town of Stark, once run by a TM and now owned by Ops. Stark was an abandoned desert town where a TM named Colleen Colletta ran an underground facility to capture and torture child molesters and abusers . . . and unfortunately some others that were either relatively innocent or had already paid for the crime . . . like his late wife, Bam. The topside was several abandoned buildings. All the living facilities were underground. He wore a white hoodie with a picture of Iron Man over jeans and white sneakers.

He was there with a man named Mark Meachum, known as Microchip of the Neutrals, a group of low-level, subconscious channelers that worked unofficially from time to time with Ops.

Approximately forty and a former native of Florida, Mark was about thirty pounds overweight. He had wavy black hair, a mustache, dark blue eyes, and chubby cheeks. As the tech expert of the team, he was used to sitting around hacking while eating potato chips. He wore a pink sweatshirt with a picture of the Pink Panther on it over black pants, and he also wore white sneakers.

Mark entered and said, "Let's go to the lab."

"Great," muttered Sam, feeling the pull in his legs as he swung them out to get off the sofa.

Once in the lab, Mark recalled the graphs on the blood tests and said, "I've gotten back results on that bloodwork I took a while back. Now, keep in mind, I'm not an expert, but these are fairly standard tests and generally accurate, especially given the prevalence of the condition in our society."

"Condition?" asked Sam.

Mark nodded and said seriously, "You appear to have symptoms of polymyalgia rheumatica or rheumatoid arthritis."

Sam frowned. "Arthritis? I'm only 51."

"But you're in the range for both. PMR is rare under 50, but the muscle pains in your arms, legs, and neck are distinctive from other ailments. The soreness in your wrist, knee, and base of the neck, however, are more typical of rheumatoid arthritis."

"Well, I have been beat up a bit over the years, but certainly not as much as an average football player."

Mark shook his head. "PMR and RA are both auto-immune diseases. Your body gets confused and attacks itself, attacks the synovial lining in the joints that cushion movement. Mostly likely, you have RA. The RA could cause the muscle soreness. I'm not a doctor, so I can't say for sure. Anyhow, the joints thus swell, but there can be other effects as well, especially the fatigue."

"And here I thought I was just getting old . . . or worn out from being Public Enemy Number one."

Sam had been framed by the TM Amy Dayne, posting as now President-Elect Shy Strong, for an attack on her on July 4, putting him on the run.

"Nope. Anyhow, there's no cure, Sam, but it's a manageable condition."

"No cure? I have to feel older than fucking Jameson the rest of my life?"

Mark laughed. "No, no. Prednisone works well on PMR and RA, and methotrexate works well on RA. If not, there's more advanced drugs, but those really hamper the immune system. You will have good and bad days, unless your system turns itself off. That sometimes happens. PMR in particular usually only lasts a year or two. RA is chronic."

Sam's eyes nearly fell out of his head. "A year or two? I don't have a year or two to feel like this!"

"Well, you'll feel better in soon, maybe just a day or two. But you'll probably need the prednisone for a while. You don't have much of a choice."

Sam fell silent, contemplating this news. Then he asked, "What caused it?"

"No one knows. There's hereditary links, but there's also theories something happens that actives the immune system and it gets confused. Anyhow, the immune system is efficient. The cartilage and other key joint and muscle parts get destroyed. The meds are there to slow it down and hope it quits."

Sam leaned against the cabinet and said, "Well . . . well, fuck me."

"We need a CT scan of your lungs as well. RA is usually known for damaging joints, but it can affect the eyes, and other organs, notably the lungs."

"I can't just walk into Sharp care and get a CT scan," said Sam dryly.

"I know that. I might have equipment here that can do it. Anyhow, that's not urgent. The more urgent item is to get the meds."

"I'm sure Theresa can do that for us."

"Okay. I'll make the contact."

Sam sighed. "How goes the rest of the work?"

Mark shook his head. "Having a stable base to work from helps. Let's take a walk."

Sam nodded. He was stiff and sore, but the exercise sometimes helped. They walked to an elevator that ascended to an empty building. Then they walked onto the California desert. It was only nine in the morning and November, so it was cool, about forty degrees. There was nothing but sand, and to the far west the hills of the Cleveland National Forest, which separated the desert from San Diego.

Mark said, "When our team has talked, for the most part we threw out the idea of proving Shy Strong is not Shy Strong. But I'm rethinking that. After all, as your failed Batman attempt proved, we can't beat her in combat. And we don't have to prove she's Amy Dayne. If we just prove she is *not the person she claims to be*, she can be removed from office."

"Right."

"Now that Strong or Dayne or whatever you want to call her has won, time is valuable."

"I prefer to call her skank-bitch from Hell, but we can call her Dayne for now."

"Shank and Little Jack are worried. There's already movement in Washington to cut the budget for Ops and the WSA in half. That would cripple Ops, though most of the WSA funding is from the Consortium and Shank would make political waves. He's really our best partner right now. He likes a good fight."

Sam laughed. "Yeah, no shit."

"Shank's intel was invaluable to us," said Mark. "I've learned something, but I don't know how it helps us. We knew from the beginning whoever Strong replaced had to be genetically close for the glamour to work. A TM can't just impersonate anyone They basically alter on a subtle level their own genetic traits and aura to modify their appearance to look usually younger, though sometimes older, or make subtle changes in aging.

"Basically, without Strong's corpse, we've found no trace of Strong's DNA. Dayne had brothers and a father, and their DNA is on record. Tracking that, we've found Dayne's father is *not* her biological father. The brothers definitely related to the man posing as Dayne's father. But he was probably her stepfather. Strikes me as one of those 'family secret' type things no one ever found out about," said Mark. They were walking along an old railroad line, and now turned back towards Stark.

Sam was quiet for a minute, then said, "Well, I agree, I don't really know how that helps us."

"I know . . . the problem is logistics. Even if we had bulletproof evidence, putting it through the process would still take weeks, or more likely months. I don't know if we'll be able to pull this off. Ops has indicated Geneva has had some success finding a way to stop Quotient. This may well now be our only hope."

"True. I mean, even if we stop Dayne, we don't know that it will stop the Consortium's Mars plan, especially now that they've established a city. We're probably . . . shit. At this point, I get the feeling we're the Alfred to Ops' Batman."

Mark just nodded.

Before he could continue, Sam pointed at camera nine and said, "Theresa is back. I should go talk to her."

"Of course. I'll go back to research and Hershey's bars."

Sam laughed and said, "Have fun."

He exited and made his way via an elevator to the surface of Stark, which was at this point entirely semi-collapsed buildings except for the old Western bar. Inside, it was a shambles, but there was a clear spot behind the bar where a trapdoor in the floor led to a very secure cubby. Only the right bio and aural metrics could get a person through the trapdoor.

Sam lifted it up and found Theresa approaching, carrying three plastic shopping bags from Stater Brothers.

"Shopping sucks," said Theresa.

Sam laughed, and as Theresa put the bags down on the sandy floor, they kissed gently.

Carlotta Brussels was always Carla in her hometown of Cincinnati, Ohio, but after leaving there when she was eighteen, she went by her middle name of Theresa. Picked up by Finley, a guy leaving New York for Vegas to recover from 9/11, on July 12, 2002, she left Ohio and her crazy mother forever.

Thirty-six-year-old Theresa was five-six and now 138 pounds, having put on a few pounds in recent years, mostly in her hips and butt. She was pretty average in terms of weight and appearance for someone of her age, with a decent figure despite only working out once or twice a week. She was too busy to work out. She had stringy blonde hair and a pretty, slightly wrinkled face with pouting lips, freckles, and oddly cold, deep blue eyes.

She had left home with a man and arrived in Vegas in 2002. Sixteen months later, he dumped her. After a tumultuous year, she was mentored by a vice cop in Vegas and joined the force. Eventually, she became the Vegas PD liaison with Ops, and in 2019 transferred and joined Ops directly as a non-paranormal field agent.

When Sam had been set up by Shy Strong and turned into public enemy number one, Theresa had risked her career to get him a gem that was key to Sam's plans. They had spent some time together on a field op in 2019 and had sex, but their relationship didn't seem all that serious, though they both knew there was potential.

This was despite Sam's difficult romantic past. He'd been a loner much of his life until he met Bam Grant here in Stark on a mission in 2007. They married, but she was murdered by the TM Shanna McGruder in 2014. That had led to Sam's romance with Meredith Patience a couple years later, which ended when Meredith was blasted into a parallel dimension in January of 2018 and presumed dead. Ops later learned she survived, but she was subsequently killed by Calico's Consortium team in May without Sam ever seeing her again.

On September 17, Theresa had been on a mission with a nonparanormal field operative named Myke Kozlowski. He'd wound up eaten by a tiger. That had made Theresa rethink a lot about her life, especially since Koz was from Cleveland and she had to make a journey back to Ohio for his funeral.

She had gone downstate and visited her mother.

It didn't go well.

She'd been back for a month, and they'd basically been friends with benefits during that time.

Today Theresa wore khaki shorts and a white T-shirt with a red fist stenciled on it and green sandals. Sam took the bags and said, "Any trouble?"

"Only with the prices. Even with the price of gas, I should go into San Diego. They rob you blind out here in the desert," she muttered.

Sam laughed. "Those hiding out in holes in the ground can't be choosers."

"At least I got your mint chocolate chip ice cream. Although how you can eat that shit is beyond me."

"It's God's greatest gift, other than you."

She rolled her eyes. "It's too early in the day to be drinking, dude."

"Actually, I could use one. Mark had some bad news. Can we talk?"

Looking like she'd been punched, she said, "Sure."

They put the groceries away quickly and went to the recreation room as Sam said, "This place disturbingly reminds me of the basement of my home as a kid in Racine."

"It has that leftover 80s look," said Theresa, playing a fake violin.

There was a large screen built-in television and several faux windows showing the desert outside. The room had white carpeting and gray walls, a large light brown sofa, two leather chairs, a coffee table, and several paintings on the wall of various famous landmarks like the Eiffel tower.

Sam sat on the sofa, Theresa to his left, sitting with her back against the short end to face him. Worriedly, she said, "What's he found? Someone find us? Time to go on the run? Do I pack up our condos in Vegas?"

"No, nothing like that. It's all the stiffness I've had. Turns out, I'm not just an old fucker."

He could see the worry on her face, despite her effort to hide it, and quickly explained. As he did so, she looked a little more relaxed, but also confused.

Concluding, he said, "I need meds for a few weeks to see what happens."

"Well, I can work on that. But . . . I mean, how are you?"

Sam sighed. "Mostly pissed off. This somewhat takes me out of the game. I'm physically shot. And I have a feeling those few weeks I need to get better is time we are not going to get, now that Strong officially won."

"Yeah, I'm with you there," she said.

"You still look worried."

Theresa smiled. "I like you, Sam. I'm upset you're hurt, and I don't know what to do for you."

"Just be there for me."

She smiled. "I'm not good at the nurse Nightwing shit."

"That's Nightingale. Nightwing is the guy Dick Grayson became after he gave up being Robin back in the 80s."

"Whatever." She put a hand on him. "Let's go to bed. I bet I can make you feel better for at least ten minutes."

"You're optimistic," he said with a laugh. Then he said, "You know, we never have talked much about Ohio. You've been a lot quieter since the trip there."

She narrowed her eyes. "It didn't go well."

"Do you want to talk about it?"

Looking around like a cornered cat, she said, "I had a difficult relationship with my mom. That's why I left home with Finley when I was eighteen." She had filled in Sam on her history some time ago. "After Koz . . . after that . . . horrible day, I thought maybe I should make peace with her."

"I see."

Theresa shook her head. "I learned you can only make peace with someone if they want it as well. Mostly, we said nothing and then started screaming."

"I'm sorry."

She shook her head. "I don't think that's really bothering me. What's bothering me is how Koz died. That . . . was horrible."

"Well, it's not much, but the M.E. said the initial strike broke his neck. He was dead before he hit the ground."

Glaring at him, she said, "That *doesn't* help."

"I know . . . he was my friend, you know, but I couldn't even go to the funeral thanks to fucking Dayne. I brought him into Ops. He was very capable, but we don't exactly train to fight hand-to-hand with wild animals."

"Yeah."

Sam sensed the mood and was about to suggest they get an early lunch or a late breakfast when one of his thirteen clandestine phones rang. He saw immediately it was Jameson and said, "I have to take this. It's Jon."

"Sure," said Theresa, and suddenly she was alert and concerned.

"Old man?" said Sam.

"Takes one to know one. We need to talk."

"Are you pregnant?"

Jameson laughed. "No. But this is the only news that could be more surprising. Jennifer Saunders is awake."

Chapter Six
The Mystery of Osa
November 6, 2020

"Are you always this energetic?" asked Medina of Colin.

Colin was brushing his teeth and shaving at the same time, a notable feat, in their Cairo, Egypt, motel room. "But of course."

Geneva arrived, having gone down the hall to get ice. She took one look at her sister and her jaw fell. "You have got to be kidding me! You look like a leftover from a British Colonial Empire movie!"

"I was going more for Indiana Jones," said Medina. She wore baggy explorer pants, a white shirt, and a straw hat with her hair pinned up underneath it.

Geneva slapped her forehead. "What about *undercover* don't you understand?"

At that moment, Colin stepped out of the bathroom. He wore a bright orange blazer, yellow T-shirt, and black pants with loafers. Geneva pointed at him and said to her sister, "You stand out more than *him* in that thing!"

"But it's neat, and besides, our contact knows who we are!"

"But we could be followed!"

Medina threw up her hands.

Geneva looked at Colin and said, "You aren't exactly blending in either!"

"My dear child, I am a master thespian. Should the need arise, I could pose as a homeless immigrant from Calcutta or the President of the United States! But there is no need at the moment."

"The Consortium is everywhere, Colin."

"Exactly!" he said, and he put a finger on her nose and said, "Which is why Medina and I will make ourselves conspicuous and roam the city while you get the information we need."

"Hey, I'm not here as fluff," said Medina.

Geneva immediately added, "That was not the plan. If you change the plan, it has to be discussed with us!"

He pointed at the ceiling and his watch, then said, "You are merely women. You learn only when you need to know."

"Aghhhhh!" shouted Medina, and she threw a pillow at him.

Meanwhile, he typed a text he didn't send that said simply:

WE'RE BUGGED. AGENTS DOWNSTAIRS TOO

Geneva and Medina both noticed the text on his watch and nodded.

Playing the role, Geneva said, "You are a masculine asshole, Ridgeway. If I didn't need you, I'd leave you here with the bill!"

"Fortunately, I'm here to do the planning and thinking for you. You're lucky I don't take you over my lap and spank you for your lack of forethought. Imagine assuming the Consortium wouldn't have agents here! Such careless thought has brought down empires!"

Medina said, "C'mon, sis, you go on. I'll make the sexist jerk here at least buy me lunch."

"A truly empowered woman would buy her own lunch," said Colin.

She threw another pillow at him.

Eight minutes later, after Medina put on more blush and a brighter shade of pink lipstick and Colin changed into more sensible clothes — he left on the yellow T-shirt but covered it with a black jacket and put on socks and white and black sneakers — they exited.

As expected, they were followed. Medina whispered to Colin as they exited onto the congested, curved ramp leading to the lobby, "We've got two at nine o'clock."

"And one at three."

"I read. And one at 4:30."

"We're quite popular," said Colin with a manic smile. Then he started waving his hand and snapping his fingers. "Taxi!"

Colin fumbled with directions, but Medina simply showed the driver a photo of the contact point, the Armed Forces Hospital. Geneva had set up appointments with two contacts, but her real contact was the second. Medina and Colin were going to see the *fake* contact, who was really a WSA agent named Sid Lahibri, who was actually from New York and more familiar with the Mets than the Armed Forces or anything in Egypt.

They entered the taxi.

Medina scrolled her phone. "No aura detectors."

"They may be screened or may be non-paranormal agents."

"Well, they're not going to bother us here. But what if they attack us in the hospital?" Medina asked.

"Then we thoroughly berate them and beat them into submission," said Colin, watching the road.

"Great plan," said Medina, making a face.

"Your sarcasm is lost on me. All I hear are compliments."

"It's a fine question," said Sid, studying Colin's phone and pretending to be interested. They were in an office at the hospital.

Medina sat on a chair, texting her mom various notes on cooking chili. Colin studied a diagram of the circulatory system.

Sid was a thin, bald man with a tired look, who looked more like a harangued butler than a doctor, other than wearing a white coat over his gray suit. He worked on his computer.

After thirteen minutes, Colin said, "We haven't been attacked. Odd. Come along, Miss Medina."

"Right," she said. On the way out, she said, "Nice to meet you, Sid."

"Sure. Come back for dinner if you can."

"Right-o."

Once outside, they proceeded to the lobby. Colin was glaring now, looking angry or constipated. Medina also was staring intently, but discreetly.

Finally, he said, "Nothing."

"I agree."

Colin called for a taxi. "I wonder where they went?"

Medina said worriedly, "Maybe they were onto us all along. Maybe they pretended to follow us just so they could follow sis."

Geneva allowed Medina and Colin a forty-minute head start. She wore a long robe, but one carefully designed to allow her to not trip if she had to run. Her robe was dark blue, and she had tucked the hair longer than the robe into the back of the robe. She'd discarded make-up, other than using some provided to colin to darken her skin.

Under her robe, she wore Kevlar. The only item that could give her away were her boots. The robe mostly hid them, but they were solid black boots. Still, after walking a bit, they were covered in dust and didn't stand out. She had no choice. She had to protect her feet.

Extremely wary, she exited the hotel and took three taxis and walked three miles to make sure she wasn't followed. She wasn't. But due to the delays, it was nearly 11 in the morning when she reached Al-Arafa, a slum that dated back nearly 1500 years.

Cairo had a metropolitan population of around twenty million, making housing difficult. Al-Arafa was known as the City of the Dead, a necropolis where the living had taken up living among the deceased. There was limited electricity and sanitation.

The area looked like a slum. All of the buildings were low lying, and many were in a state of advanced dilapidation, although some were painted yellow or pink, mixing with the dilapidation in a bizarre fashion.

The result was a winding, twisting maze and a terrible smell. Geneva had researched the area and worn nose filters, but her primary concern was basic sanitation. She couldn't wear gloves without standing out, so she was extremely careful to touch nothing. She had also smuggled a box of sanitized wipes in her robe.

Finding her way around the streets would have been impossible without the map her contact, Amenhotep, had sent her. She tried to mark her progress in case she lost her phone, not wanting to be lost if she were attacked and couldn't use the map. Besides, she was very wary of being followed.

But she saw no one.

Moving to her contact point, she realized it was a pink building. Geneva avoided a dead dog and entered a dark room. Although she didn't know any Egyptian dialects — she'd worked most of her Ops career in Russian and Europe and never really had the need to learn it — her contact had given her sufficient background to maneuver.

But he wasn't here.

"You're safe here."

Geneva whirled to attack, but instead she found a woman standing before her with her hands raised. She wore a long robe similar to Geneva's, though purple. She had a long but attractive face with interestingly contrasted oval eyes that were dark brown. She was wearing make-up, something to make her supple lips look moist. Her long hair was so black it looked blue in the sunlight outside the building.

Before Geneva could strike, and Geneva hesitated because the woman had her arms up, she said, "I'm not here to hurt you. We must talk! Please understand that!"

Geneva was in defensive stance and said, "That's good, because I've been at this a long time, and I can defend myself. Who are you?"

"I am Osa Carrera, Consortium and INN double-agent. I am working with Amenhotep, but he can't help you with your inquiry. He is still at the university. You are Geneva Kane, correct?"

"Of course. How did you follow me?"

With her hands still up, Osa said hurriedly, "I didn't. I waited for you in here because this facility was modified by my allies to be completely bug-proof. There were agents on your tail. I have dispatched them, so we can talk in private in here, but we must talk *fast*. My partner — not my real partner, one of the Consortium agents following your team — got knocked off by a cart, so we've got about eight to nine minutes before I have to leave to make sure he doesn't find this place."

"Who are you? What do you want?"

"We're almost out of time to stop Calico Kelkirk. I admire you, Geneva, always have form afar. To be brief, I was part of the Society of Jacks due to my parents being upper echelon members. I was part of the upper echelon but turned my back on them. There are others inside the Society in the same position. Anyhow, I joined INN and keep the post as it's a huge resource of inside information we hope to use to take the Society down. And it also gives me access to the world."

"Why talk to me? What do you want? I thought INN and the Consortium were rivals." Geneva was remaining firmly in defensive mode, but Osa had kept her hands up, knowing Geneva was wary.

"They were," she said, nodding firmly. "But that changed. When Hart died, there was a vacuum at the top of INN. Hart thought he had the line of succession settled. He did not. Nature abhors a vacuum. At the same time, Kelkirk eliminated his main rivals in the Consortium by stopping the late Kosar's COVID-19 plan."

"I had fun wrecking that plan," said Geneva with a broad smile.

Osa smiled. "I can imagine! Kelkirk wound up at the top of the pyramid, and INN has slowly and silently been largely absorbed by the Consortium. I was a part of this, being a Society member and an INN employee. That far I was willing to go. This was before I found out the true nature of Calico Kelkirk's plans."

"Can we stop her?" asked Geneva.

"Yes. I think so. But you can't go to anyone to find out about the sword. Calico *will* find out. And you must stop her. There are ways to stop Quotient. She has been quietly gathering up key people for over a year now."

"We know that."

Osa curtly shook her head. "No, she started *before* you made your moves. You just made her move faster. But there are key members of the Consortium sprinkled inside the Society. Some of us are working to stop her from the inside. I do know she is afraid of *something*. But trust no one."

"Except you?" asked Geneva with a sardonic grin.

Osa just smiled.

"Why come to me now?"

"Your being here is going to tip off Calico that you're up to something. And they will know you were here. Using INN, they know almost everything that happens. A fly can crap on a wall in Pittsburgh, and they know instantly."

"The sword is useful?"

"I have no idea. But *something* is. Just trust only Ops. I can tell you, I have very high information from one of my fellow agents working to bring them down from the inside, and Ray was the only double-agent we know of in your organization. You are safe there. You are safe nowhere else."

"Wait! Wait, wait, wait. You're saying Ray Coulors was working for Calico?"

Osa looked pained. "I . . . I'm sorry. I thought you had figured that out. Yes, he was, and had been for at least a few months. He died during the portal to Mars."

Geneva was astonished, but she recovered quickly. "Very well. I'll . . . deal with that later." She nodded. "If we stop Quotient, does that stop Calico?"

"Yes. This much I know — transporting humanity to Mars on the scale she seeks is *only possible with Quotient*. The sacrifice of Portland got their core group. If they could never move again, they might survive. But they need more, and the eco-system is fragile. They need Quotient to get back and forth. Stopping Quotient stops Mars and that stops their insanity."

"Where does Shy Strong fit in?"

Osa smiled. "She's a bitch, isn't she?"

Geneva nodded. "We know she's Consortium."

Osa sighed. "She's more than that, much more, but I don't know exactly what. You know she's really a paranormal named Amy Dayne, correct?" Geneva nodded, so Osa continued. "She's part of a very powerful group right at the top called the Quartet. But she's not an immediate problem. Her main role comes later. She can be in a place to do some legal maneuvering and serve as a distraction. Example one: a month ago, while you were chasing her and trying to kill her, the UN quietly passed a resolution giving entities the right to claim land rights on Mars. The Consortium claim was filed within thirty minutes."

"Damn."

"We're almost out of time."

Geneva nodded. "You're risking your life talking to me."

Osa smiled thinly. "I am a channeler, Geneva, not a TM. The Society, which you know is mostly Consortium controlled, at one point suspected my . . . sincerity. For seventeen days, I was bound to a chair nude and given random, periodic electrical shocks throughout my body. Most people tortured in this fashion are driven insane. I was the only person that never confessed. I did it because I had to, because it cemented my credibility and ability to work within. I am not afraid to die. But I am covered here, as are you. You should get your sister and that British clown out of here, however, as soon as possible."

"We will. Is there any way to contact you?"

"PO Box 509020 Anaheim. Nothing electronic. Our side is working its own methods, but I don't think we can stop Calico without help. It's why I'm coming to you now. You are the one person Calico respects . . . and fears."

Geneva nodded. "Very well. I appreciate your efforts to save the world."

"I know the Kanes. I know you will do everything to stop her. But you have to do the *right* things, not everything. I must go. You need to injure me."

Geneva immediately channeled wind and slammed Osa into a wall. Osa put out her left hand to brace herself and her wrist broke.

Then Geneva raced past. She knew by acting immediately it would take Osa by surprise and look legit. As she passed by, Osa was groaning. Geneva said, "I'm sorry, my friend."

"I did ask for it. Fare well, Miss Kane."

Geneva raced outside and went right, right, then left, reversing her path to the building.

Osa waited for a time in the rubble, her heart racing, adrenaline pumping, and her wrist throbbing. The adrenaline was dulling much of the pain, but not all of it.

The memory of her torture had come back during her telling of the tale, and it bothered her. She had not lied. The Society had used that interrogation technique on many, and they all confessed or went insane within a week, ten days at most. Her durability had given her inside access even most upper echelon members didn't have and made her trust beyond question.

Laura Jabar, her torturer, and Calypso Fernandez, the assassin, had both recruited her, once it was clear she was in an important position and horrified by the soul-slaughter being used by Calico.

Dragging herself up, she headed back to her partner, ignoring the crowd, hoping she had won and success was achieved.

Chapter Seven
Betrayal
November 6-7, 2020

The mission a failure, Geneva's thoughts were racing as she returned to the hotel. The double-surprise of Osa and Ray's double-agent status left her almost sick to her stomach. On the one hand, she had gained a valuable ally in Osa, someone deep on the inside. But on the other . . . Ray. Ray?

Frist things first. When she arrived, Colin and Medina had not returned, but Medina had sent a text that they'd had no interruptions so were stopping for lunch. She called Colin.

"Is this line secure?" she asked.

"Most certainly," he confirmed. She could hear the noise of an outdoor restaurant in the background, which she figured would stifle any of their conversation.

"We have to get out of town. I just had contact with . . . someone. We need to move fast."

"Very well. I have multiple flights booked to return myself and Miss Medina to Germany to meet with, ah, the metalurologist."

Geneva laughed. "I don't think that's a word, but I get what you mean. Can you get me on a flight to Siberia quietly and quickly?"

"Close enough. I'll work on it. What's going on?"

"I'll explain more later. I just want out of town. This is a dead-end. Text me the flight details."

"As you wish, m'dear. Good health."

He hung up. She then called Little Jack on his private cell.

"Geneva? What's wrong?" he asked, knowing only an emergency would cause her to use his private line.

"I've run into major complications. I'm heading back to Siberia as if I were never here. When I get there . . . we have to talk and in a very secure way. I don't even want Joy to know."

Pause. "Okay. Sure, whatever you need."

"Good. Figure tomorrow."

"Hey, I'll be here. It's the job."

"The task in Cairo was a failure. My contact was intercepted by someone we thought we knew. INN reporter Osa Carerra," said Geneva on the phone from Siberia at around six in the evening. That made it the middle of the night in Las Vegas.

"Whoa," said Little Jack. He was sitting in the waterbed in the Ops' condo he shared with Joy, who was still asleep.

"Yeah, no kidding," said Geneva. She was in the control room in the cave in Siberia, looking at a series of colored graphs on screens. Despite wearing a black winter coat, black pants, and white thigh-high boots, she was chilly. They were cutting back on the heat to help conserve resources.

"The other news is about . . . about Ray. These issues are intertwined. Is . . . would you be offended if we linked in Sam?"

"No, although it's the middle of the night here. He might be pissed." Little Jack laughed. "Anyone else?"

"Not for the moment."

Little Jack needed about six minutes to link in Sam from Stark. Sam looked tired. He wore a black and red checkered, flannel jacket and was sitting in front of a computer in the server room. His hair and beard were a mess.

"You realize you're taking away valuable comic book reading time, right?" he asked.

Geneva said, "Ah, Sam . . . I truly regret making this call for that reason . . . and many others."

Frowning, Sam said, "What's going on?"

Geneva sighed. "Gentlemen, my mission to Cairo to get info was a bust. I never met my contact. That's because I was intercepted by a woman we know. Osa Carerra."

"Whoa!" said Sam.

"That's what *I* said," said Little Jack.

"And that's how I felt when I saw her in the slums," said Geneva. "But she gave me quite a bit of info in the few minutes we had." Geneva quickly recapped the basics and added, "So based on her statements, I immediately returned to Siberia to work with the team here."

"Carerra is a double-agent . . . interesting," said Sam, rubbing his chin.

"You know of her outside of INN?" asked Geneva.

"No. But she's been one of the go-to interviewers for Dayne-Strong-Whatever during her campaign. If she's coming to you now, something big is imminent," said Sam.

"I'd agree," added Little Jack.

"My concern is she's . . . I don't know, that this is some type of ruse," said Geneva thoughtfully.

"It could be, but I don't know what she would gain, other than delay your getting information," said Sam.

"Yeah, but that might be exactly what they need. Maybe the damned sword can stop the Big Blob and they wanted to slow us down," said Little Jack. "And trickery is easier than trying to steal it from Geneva, who we all know is one of the premier paranormals in the world."

"Thank you, flattery is accepted," said Geneva with a smile.

"So . . . how can we find out if Osa is genuine?" asked Sam.

"That's what I'm asking you two," said Geneva. "Because . . . there's something else."

"Well, it's not good, is it?" said Sam, sensing her hesitancy.

"No . . . no." She paused. "Osa says . . . Ray . . . Ray Coulors . . . was working for Calico's people."

Sam surprised her, because he showed no surprise. Little Jack did a double-take. "Ray?"

"Yes."

Sam nodded. "I didn't know Ray well, but we haven't heard from him since Portland. That isn't unusual for unofficial operatives. Still . . . it concerned me. And he is the type who could fall for their more benign features and go his own way . . . damn."

"I'm not sure what Ray might have told them, how exposed we are," said Geneva worriedly.

"Not that much. Ray wasn't officially with Ops," said Little Jack quickly. "He worked with us from time to time, but he didn't know anything important, just like the other M-Men." The M-Men were low-level channelers that helped Ops by seeking out vampires and totem pushers in the Midwest. "He knew nothing the Consortium couldn't have found out on their own."

"Osa said he died during the Portland thing. I don't know where his body is," said Geneva sadly.

"Well, there's nothing we can do about that," said Little Jack.

Sam added, "Agreed, and we have only Osa's word, which while I believe it, it's still second-hand knowledge. I don't know of a way to test Osa, but I believe she's on the up-and-up. She took a lot of risk to talk to you. She didn't have to tell you about Ray, either. It would benefit her to keep that secret if she were trying to bluff you."

"I think so, too."

"Okay, well, we just have to be very secure," said Little Jack. "I mean, what else can we do?"

Neither Sam nor Geneva had any other ideas.

Chapter Eight
Alliances
November 14-15, 2020

"Failure now would negate all of our achievements," said Calico Kelkirk to her mentor and, now that had her father had passed away in January, most important friend, John Englehart, via her Skype-like app.

"True."

Calico leaned back in the office chair in the sterile office in her German mansion. Englehart was linked in via the app. He was in Hollywood, working on his television show, where he had been since the events in Portland. Calico, Yellow and Smith had been moving back and forth with Quotient's aid when needed, which wasn't often, and Trixie had been completely on Mars, primarily occupied with medical reviews of all the new citizens.

"So, I believe meting Saunders is worth it."

"Perhaps."

They were both silent. Calcio slouched in the chair, fatigued. Thirty-one-year-old Calico had chestnut brown hair, long and straight, parted in the middle. Her eyes were blue and narrow. Her face was thin, and her body was very thin except for a clearly artificially enhanced chest. She spoke in a clearly American accent — fitting as she was born and raised by her mother's best friend in the Detroit area before Kelkirk came and brought her to Germany. She wore a white sweater with red stars, jeans, and brown boots, looking decidedly casual.

"That sounds less than committed," said Calico, arching an eyebrow.

"Indeed," said Englehart, who was always called simply by his last name as he despised the name John. Now sixty-one, Englehart was as energetic as he had been as a young man. Most of that was due a brutal schedule that involved balancing time with the Consortium and the Society against running his own Hollywood action show, *Fire Johnson At Large*, now in its fifth season. He was a large man, now weighing a solid 270 as he was overweight, but also tall at six feet and four inches. With a curly blond beard and blond hair that showed only the smallest signs of aging, he looked much younger. Stylish glasses helped him appear bookwormish and inquisitive . . . accurate traits, but ones that hid a strong urge to save the world.

Calico looked at the pictures on the gray walls of the office, pictures of German mountains in the snow. It was a far prettier picture than Detroit. In Germany, it was nine at night on Saturday, November 14. It was mid-day in Los Angeles, where Englehart was working in his home office with the sun shining through the window on his desk, lighting up his Disney character figurines.

"Very well. Let's summarize, shall we?" asked Calico

"It's always best. I've learned through many years of writing a summary is always good when disorganized."

"I would not say we are disorganized. I would say we are indecisive."

He cocked his head. "Valid. Continue, dear."

She put her hands in her lap and twiddled her thumbs as she spoke. "Our Mars plan took a major ramp forward in March of 2018. That's when Courtney and the portal gems enabled us access into all of the tunnels of Special Ops, and we cleared out their entire trove of alien gems and technology. Among those gems were supremely advanced portal gems. We also found a destroyed tachyon well on the alien ship. It was in hundreds of pieces, but father was able to use the information he gained as leader of the Consortium — the information known by the alien Lexx which father downloaded before Lexx was taken to Atlantia by Marrina and Ops in '16 — to rebuild it. The tachyon well made very precise, controlled teleportation possible. That enabled us to build the first Mars colony and establish the city and prison colony. But the tachyon well burned out, so by earlier this year, we were back to using the stolen portal gems."

"But around that time is when we found Quotient in the ice in Antarctica," he said.

"Correct." She pursed her lips. "Quotient has unlimited teleportational ability. He is some type of alien that is essentially a sentient mass of tachyonic and anti-matter influx, from what I've learned. But we don't know his nature. We do not know if his power has limits or if he's immortal or what he'll do if he decides to go to a soccer game on Pluto and leave us."

"In which case, we're back to using portal gems, which are viable, though difficult," said Englehart. "Or fix the tachyon well."

"The tachyon well is beyond repair. As for the gems, we don't know their limits, and we also have no way to obtain more, now that Ops, at least according to our sources, knows their complex was pilfered."

Englehart sensed her direction and said, "I worry about Saunders, Calico. This is a risk. This is, I suspect, a ploy."

"Perhaps. But she is incredibly smart, given Clegg is stuck in her head. And she's brilliant. She might help us."

"Or betray us."

"I won't give her that chance."

"How will you ensure that?" asked Englehart with a mix of surprise and curiosity.

She told him.

He nodded and said, "Very well, Calico. I trust you. I have always trusted and loved you."

"Of course. And I you. We have been through much together, and we will weather this storm as well. I'll instigate contact with Saunders."

"Very well. Keep me in the loop. I have a Society meeting, but mostly I'll be here. My script editor is hooked on oxycodone, so I'm rewriting our last three stories. And since we sacrificed the Oregon home to Quotient, I'm stuck here where people can find me with annoying questions."

"I'm sorry."

"I'm just teasing . . . mostly. By the by, any indication of Ops cracking the shell company game and getting back to me?"

Calico laughed. "They have more chance of finding a stripper in a convent than finding that house was yours." She paused. "I should get to work. Good luck."

"And to you."

Calico signed off. Then she snapped her fingers and projected her thoughts to Quotient.

In a yellow haze, the yellowish-white blob appeared between her and the ceiling, rotating like a spinning top, then stabilizing. It stared at her.

She said simply, "My friend, we have a job to do."

The next evening, Calico said to Jennifer Saunders, "I appreciate your agreeing to this time and place."

"It is a bit odd," said Jen, looking around.

They were inside a new zoo being built outside Detroit. For the most part, the zoo was finished. It was expected to open in the spring, March 1, and as a result most of the final work was just decorative items like covering wiring, painting, and putting in fixtures.

They were leaning on a brown chain-link fence that overlooked a rocky enclosure that would house turtles. The only sound was that of birds.

It was Sunday, November 15, so there was no work occurring. The evening was mostly cloudy, cold, and windy. Calico wore a brown leather jacket with black pants and boots, the wind blowing her hair. Detroit time, it was six, and the lights from the construction area provided the only light in the area. It was rather dark. Jen wore a black flight jacket, jeans, and white sneakers. Human robot Radar wore jeans, a black T-shirt with a picture of the American flag on it, and old sneakers. The wind blew everyone's hair.

Quotient hovered above them.

This did not make Jen or Radar happy.

"Odd? I suppose. I thought it best to meet in America. I grew up not far from here. I knew this place would be quiet."

Jen smiled. "And there's plenty of places for you to hide agents."

Calico leaned her arms on the railing. Jen did the same. Calico turned to her left to look at Jen and said, "Quotient is the only agent I need. I am amazed you survived the attack on the island, though pleased. It was *never* our intent to cause harm. I'm sorry about Miss Patience and Miss Jordan."

Jen bristled, but she relented and let Oscar take control of the body and the conversation. Oscar-Jen said, "I . . . I understand. Believe me, that's the only reason I'm willing to talk. I'm not angry. I understand better now what you want . . . and I can help." She nodded at Radar. "One point of agreement. Radar goes where I say. He's my bodyguard . . . it's a point Ops insists on. His real self was destroyed some time ago, so he's just a consciousness that switches between robots. And besides being bodyguard, he can help crunch numbers."

Calico gave a sly smile. Jen felt nervous. Finally, Calico said, "He's quite an achievement. The work of Zaborski?"

"Nah, I built myself in my basement," said Radar, smiling but his eyes had a warning stare.

Calico nodded. "There is no problem with that. I have my bodyguard. You have yours. This should allow us the, well, peace of mind to converse in a productive, scientific manner. Now, how can you assist?"

"That's what I wanted to explain."

"Fine."

Suddenly, Calico turned and faced Jen and pointed. She said, "*(^*(&&%%!"

"No!" shouted Oscar-Jen.

Then they were gone.

***

"Now we can truly talk in privacy," said Calico.

Jen had shut her eyes, expecting a fight to the death with Quotient.

Instead, they were in a building in Red Kelkirkstadt. It was a bell tower and was at the edge of the Riker's dome, showing a stunning display of red Martian mountains and the endless stars of outer space.

"Whoaaaaaa."

The bell tower was empty; there was no bell. It was basically a faux wood floor with three wooden chairs and the window looking out. Quotient hovered above them. In the rafters were pigeons.

Oscar was still in control of the body. Physically, Jen sat on the chair and said, "I feel sick."

Calico sat across from her, Quotient hovering above and slightly behind her to the right. He was near a door that led to the stairway that led down to the main chapel. Radar leaned against the wall near Oscar-Jen.

"Teleportation can have that effect," said Calico sympathetically.

Oscar-Jen nodded. "I . . . I'm getting over it. Thanks for the warning."

"I felt it best for our discussion to ensure we have no prying eyes," said Calico.

"Some trip," said Radar, and she didn't notice his smile he made to himself.

Being on Mars was exactly what he had expected . . . and *needed*.

Oscar-Jen nodded. He hoped the original location gave Ops some information, but now he was on his own. Ops was light years away.

Jen was totally alone.

And if Oscar messed up, she would lose not only her life but her soul. And so would he, Anissa, and all Jen's alters.

Gesturing, Calico said, "The floor is yours."

Turning to Radar, Oscar said, "Radar, I think we need to talk privately for a bit."

"Sure." He looked at Calico. "You got a Martian Starbucks or something?"

"The room next door is empty. You may wait there." Calico quickly used a phone app to unlock it. "You may go in."

"Thanks. Call me when you're done."

Then he exited.

"How much do you know about me?" asked Oscar.

Calico arched an eyebrow and smiled, clearly mildly amused. "Mr. Clegg, you were married to Zenith for years. My father is the one who pulled her back to the TM world and away from you.[4] He created Zenith and restored her after you damaged her. I know *everything* about you. Trust me, he kept very close track of you over the years."

Bristling, Oscar said, "I see it other ways. I restored her, and he corrupted her again."

Calico put up a hand. "Enough. This serves neither of us. There is bitterness between myself and you simply because of who I am, Oscar. But I did not do those things to you, and I tell you this in all sincere truth, in his later years my father had great regret for his actions. He allowed his hatred of others to become much like them. But as Zenith drove the Earth towards inevitable doom, he fought her and found his higher purpose, to save this world. So we owe you our gratitude, which is why I honored your request to speak."

Oscar was surprised at her attitude, for he could sense her sincerity.

Anissa just said, "She's a pompous butthead."

"Hush," said Jen internally.

Oscar ignored them. "I also apologize. After all, I am not here out of anger or conflict. I am here because I know your father, regardless of his character, ah, flaws . . . knew his stuff. If he believed the world is about to end, then it's about to end."

"It is," confirmed Calico with a hint of real fear in her eyes.

"Many in Ops believe in your plan, to save humanity with a relocation to Mars. But your *method* of doing so will never allow

---

[4] Again, as told in TM 1.1 "Torture Magic"

them to admit this or assist you. I . . . am more pragmatic." He paused. "I experimented on my own people in the concentration camps. I married Zenith. I worked with aliens with Ops knowing the dangers. I am not afraid to take a risk for the greater good."

"Ironically, it was your work with Subject Six that really set all of this in motion," said Calico thoughtfully.

"What do you mean?"

"Well, by investigating her, you set into motion all the events with the parallel world. That combined with the gems has created enormous tachyonic heat that has intensified global warming a thousand-fold. Those projects of global doom by 2150 are now for 2030 and mostly . . . because of you."

In Jen's body, Oscar showed anger and aggression. "That's an *exaggeration*, to say the least."

"Perhaps. I say this not to make you feel guilty, merely to state a fact. How do you seek to assist?"

"Everyone in the world will fight you, Calico, once the secret of Quotient is known. And after Portland, that will happen eventually. Inevitably."

"Probably," she admitted.

"I can make Quotient unnecessary."

Calico's eyes widened. She tried to hide it, but she was clearly excited by this proposal. "I'll need some explanation."

Oscar-Jen nodded. "Most certainly." He took a deep breath. "It's founded on what I learned about alien technology, both during the years I studied Subject Six and much of it afterwards during the time Jennifer was in the parallel world as part of the resistance against Zenith's rule." Calico nodded understanding, so Oscar continued. "Alien spacecraft have landed on Earth for eons. Most of them are buried and never to be found. After all, nearly 80% of the world is water, and many of them made water landings to avoid human scrutiny.

"All alien spacecraft arrive here via tachyon warp drive. They basically punch a hole through space, which is why most craft that have arrived here are from far away and not, say, a planet outside

Pluto. The crash ruptures the tachyonic drive into gems, some of which retain the power to create 'blank' dimensions based on the user's conscious or subconscious thoughts, or move through localized space. A few others have much more mild powers, like the ability to enhance latent paranormal ability."

"I'm well aware of these facts, Mr. Clegg."

Oscar put up a hand. "Patience, Calico. May I?"

"Of course."

"Thank you. Calico, you must understand the full process, but I'm also an old man. If I had lived in 2004, I'd be 94 or 95 now. Hell, even I can't remember, I'm so old. Us old men tend to dodder. Being in Jen's body helps, but I'm still an old man at the end of the day."

Calico smiled politely. "It's charming. Go on."

"Ships that crash land obviously are subject to damage. But even those that landed safely decay. But if they don't, then you have a ready-made tachyon well."

"What about the psychic heat?"

"The ships can absorb that when functioning."

Calico frowned. "Father studied something like this. When Lexx's base of operations fell in Siberia in '16, father . . . I probably shouldn't tell you this . . . but father gained access to most of that data. This was Lexx's whole plan, round up the items to create a new way home, but *he* was shifting in *dimensional* space, while *we* want to shift in *local* space, but the principle is the same."

"Then you know it's feasible. And I can do the conversion for you. It was a component of our work back in the day before Subject Six woke up."

Calico shook her head. "Perhaps. He abandoned it . . . well, that's not precisely true. Father was always very cunning and had multiple methods of obtaining any goal. He'd been looking for Quotient since he stopped Zenith in Illinois in '14. In terms of the alien spaceship theory of tachyon movement, there's problems."

"Which are?"

Calico hesitated. "Primarily resources . . . but that's not the only objective."

Oscar admitted, "Yes, that could be an issue. There are ships, though the one we investigated in the parallel world was already taken to Atlantia after Ops rescued it from Necra in Africa. We'd have to find another ship."

Calico studied Oscar-Jen. "That may not be necessary. There's alternatives."

"Such as?"

Again, Calico hesitated. She finally said, "I cannot say more until I have spoken with my colleagues. Alignment with anyone in Ops is certainly something we must all be on board with for us to proceed."

"Of course."

"I would . . . appreciate it if you would merely wait here overnight while we discuss. This is the main building, where only I and my party lives. There is security, but I can get the guest services to provide your needs."

"Of course. I'm glad to stay," said Oscar, smiling thinly.

Neither of them addressed the fact that Oscar-Jen had no way to get anywhere without Calico authorizing it for Quotient. They both knew Oscar was effectively a prisoner until Calico decided what to do.

Then he might be dead.

Calico rose. "Please wait. I'll summon assistance. Let's plan to meet at six tomorrow morning American Eastern time, roughly a half-day from now. Is that acceptable?"

"I'm on Pacific Coast time, but I'll make it work," said Oscar.

Calico nodded. "It is appreciated. We can discuss our research and then I can show you the grandeur of Red Kelkirkstadt."

"I'd like that."

She smiled. "Superb. Ah, the help will be here soon. Let me show you to your room, then I will speak to your friend next door, then be about my business."

Then she exited via the door. Quotient quivered . . . and faded away.

"Whoaaaaaaaaaaa, that was intense," said Anissa internally as they arrived in a hotel room that looked like, as Geneva had once said, a

Residence Inn in Boston. But it had a glorious full- wall view of the Martian landscape, which made the décor irrelevant.

"You haven't seen the half of it yet," warned Oscar. He looked around. "At least we have a nice room."

The room Radar occupied was being redecorated, so there was no furniture other than a worktable covered in drywall tools and several folding chairs for breaks. A deck of cards sat on one of the four chairs. Radar sat on another. He had plugged into the wireless network to learn about the city. The drywall was up and pasted, but not much else had been done.

Calico knocked and said, "May I enter?"

"I'm decent," he said.

She entered, looking concerned. "Your friend and I have an agreement. I am doing some research, as is she. He." She shook her head. "Whatever. Anyhow, I thought we should speak as well."

"In regards to what topic?"

"You are a very intelligent man, Radar," she said, standing before him as he rose. She folded her arms over her chest, a subconscious effort to assert the dominant position and guard her secrets, a move Radar picked up on.

"It's been said by a few."

"It has been said you are dead."

"A ruse," he said honestly, because he had a pretty good idea that she was onto his deception of the Four Cornered Wheel and the Germans.

"Why?"

"Things are not what you think with certain people. I'm here to make sure that doesn't result in disaster."

Alarm showed on Calico's face for just a moment. "You think we're in danger?"

"I think everything is in danger. Right now, this settlement is in danger. But I'm a seer, daughter of Kelkirk," he said, making it a point to use her family name and trigger thoughts of her father and his long, brilliant knowledge. "I cannot tell you what will happen, but I can tell you what I see as a warning. That's all seers do. We receive warnings of potential outcomes to modify."

"All humans have this ability. Most humans have precognitive dreams. It does not change what happens. It merely warns them to allow them to prepare emotionally," said Calico. "At last, that's been my experience with the research."

"But I'm a channeler, which puts me on a different level."

"Accepted." She paused. "This is the only way to save humanity, moving us here. I have put my life, and my father the last years of his life, into this endeavor. *It must succeed.* There are . . . there are other plans, but all have *much* greater risk-reward ratios. Some are not even viable for decades. This must work."

"I agree, for what it's worth."

She studied him. "We are also not defenseless."

He gave a half-smile. "I've done a lot of work since I got back here — to this dimension, I mean — in June. So . . . not to alarm you or let the cat out of the bag . . . I know you built this city on a massive alien spaceship."

She cocked her head. "A theory."

"A fact. Let's not be coy."

Calico nodded. "Very well, I confirm your assumption as fact."

"But that doesn't mean you have defenses, just a great source of ready-made power."

"There are defenses."

"Are you going to tell me? Because I can tell you if they'll work. And if not, then I have time to prepare, because this is all coming to a head soon. Days, maybe even hours."

She studied him. She contemplated that he wanted to sabotage the city. But she had Quotient. Maybe Quotient couldn't eat Radar's soul, but he could melt his robot body if needed and end the threat.

"We have defenses. Come."

They used the elevator, the walked to a room that looked like a closet but was really a server room for the guest quarters. They walked quickly and without small talk. Once there, Calico entered and keyed in her personal security code.

"Observe," she said, pointing to a screen.

After twenty seconds, Radar said with astonishment. "Holy fuck-ola."

"Will that work?"

Radar laughed. "That sure the fuck will do."

"Good. Then I must return to my allies."

"Sure. I'll stay next door, in that room you're redoin' the drywall on. I don't want to get in Jen's way."

"Actually, I'd prefer you to stay elsewhere. If we are in danger, I need you in a location where you can act instantly. I've given you access to active the defense . . . unit . . . you just saw. Is that acceptable?"

Radar looked at her, and his measure of her biological stats told him she was anxious and genuinely worried about her city. "Sure."

Twenty minutes later, Calico returned to her area of the guest-quarters and met Yellow, who was wearing a white camisole and green yoga pants.

"Do not let your guard down," warned Calico of Yellow.

"I won't."

"I'll return as soon as I can. I'm going Earthside to do a little quick research, but then what we discussed in there must be discussed with Englehart in person."

"I'll handle things here. Good luck."

Calico smiled and said, "&*&*&*."

Then she and Quotient disappeared.

Chapter Nine
Layers
November 15, 2020

"Where is the fucking towel?" shouted Trixie Taylor as she groped for the pink bath towel that should have been hanging from the towel rack outside her shower in her room. She was trying to throw on the towel as the doorbell had rung.

The doorbell rang again as Trixie found it. Quickly wrapping a second, white towel around her red hair, she turned off the water and dripped all over the gray tile floor.

She went to the door and looked out the peephole. There was no one there.

"God damn it, if someone got me out of the fucking shower on a trick, I'll break their fucking necks," she muttered.

"Stop being a baby."

Trixie whirled, ready to strike, only to see Julie Julian leaning against the doorframe of the bathroom.

"Fuck! Why didn't you just portal inside?" asked Trixie.

"I was concerned I'd scare you in the shower," said Julie with a coy, sly, and sinister smile.

Trixie stared. "What do you want? You never come see me without a task."

Julie, or rather the Four Cornered Wheel, smirked.

Julie Julian had been a white, seventeen-year-old senior at Poway High, outside San Diego, when her life changed in the fall of 2017. A Christian and a big fan of Supergirl, Julie was in superb shape and was a knock-out, a ritual work-out maven.

Today, she looked just as she had three years ago. At five feet and eight inches tall, she had legs and hips of pure muscle, and a bottom that looked like a picture from a comic book. Despite her strength, she wasn't overtly muscular.

According to Ops files, Julie was always wound up and hyper. Sitting was boring. Presently, she was wearing a retro '80s hairdo. Her brown hair was teased and tightly curled, cut short but flaring wide, and swept to the right on her head. She also had dyed it to lighten the color, resulting in a few blonde streaks. Her lips were framed in light red lipstick, and her light blue eyes were highlighted by an eyelash treatment. She was wearing a blue leotard with black legs and a red hairband, having been working out in the gym on the facility while waiting for Radar to finish up.

In late 2017, Julie had been kidnapped by Trixie and taken to the Consortium, specifically Kelkirk and Calico, the father and daughter TM team running the Consortium. They had used her in a channeling experiment as a sacrifice, due to her unique affinity for the probability cloud, which was a tachyonic event that distorted probabilities in a localized field.

Julie died.

Or so most everyone thought, until she spoke to Radar on the rooftop of a building in Berlin back in the summer.

But Julie wasn't a 'her' at all. She had been consumed, the representative now of an ancient entity known as the Four Cornered Wheel.

Her outfit was the same outfit she had been wearing when ritually murdered by Kelkirk and Calico in Germany in 2017 — white boots that extended about hallway up her shin, white gloves that extended to the elbows, and a white onesie that had three circles on each side cut out. The onesie attached around her neck and fit her perfectly.

"True, Doctor Taylor, true, I again have a task for you," she said in sultry yet childish voice. Then her face went cold as stone and her voice deepened. "Our plan is greatly threatened. I have a job for you."

"I'm not your lackey," snapped Trixie, but she said it with fear.

And Julie, or more accurately the Four Cornered Wheel, knew it. Smiling and talking again in a seductive, low voice, she said in Julie's voice, "Oh, come now, Doctor Taylor. Would you like to revisit the island?"

Trixie started to shake and stepped backwards, stumbling over a pair of heels, and falling into the wall. "No! No, don't send me there!"

"I won't if you continue to accomplish your goals."

Trixie nodded quickly. Julie had shown Trixie her inevitable fate and offered to protect her from it. The island was the spot in Hell where Trixie had been held captive and tortured by the hundreds she had murdered . . . but there, she could never die.

It was a pretty powerful motivator.

"What do I do?" asked Trixie pitifully.

"Jennifer Saunders is here. This was *not* part of the plan. She is a danger to the Great Escape. She must die."

Trixie's eyes widened. "She's a powerful woman. I'm . . . can I get some help?"

"You can defeat her." Julie then gave Trixie some combat advice.

Trixie still looked very uncertain. "I don't know about this."

In a suddenly harsh and shrill voice, Julie said, "Do it or die . . . or book a ticket to the island and *never* die. Got it?"

Trixie stormed past Julie into the bathroom and removed the towel around her hair, throwing it with anger into the tub. "I should just let her win. That'd teach you."

Julie laughed a dark laugh that sounded like the cackling of Satan. "Silly child. You will go to Hell for certain unless I intervene. I can spare you that pain. Only I can do it."

Trixie snapped with obvious fear, "You lie."

"Would you risk your soul on that . . . assumption?"

Sullenly, Trixie said, "Fine. Whatever."

"Good."

"When?"

"I'll alert you when the time is right. We have to make sure Calico and Quotient aren't around and aren't coming back any time soon."

Englehart's Hollywood production office was rarely quiet. But at 10 P.M. Los Angeles time, all shooting for the day was finished, and most of the noise was from coyotes howling in the gullies that surrounded the lot.

Normally, Englehart didn't write here, for it was too easy to get pulled into production issues being on site. But on this day, he was desperate to wrap up a revised script that had been rejected from three different writers. Grumbling to himself, he was cursing the computer, which was freezing a lot.

Englehart's office had a computer on a desk under the window, which had purple shades that were pulled shut. The walls of the office were covered in pictures of Englehart with famous, infamous, and unknown Hollywood people. There were also a variety of odd trophies and an incongruously placed life-sized statue of Superman. The room was dark, other than the computer screen. Englehart wore white shorts, and red and white Hawaiian shirt, and a straw hat.

He was finishing up the end of episode three. That's when Calico and Quotient arrived in his office.

"Good Lord, warn an old man first," said Englehart as he spun in his chair and put his hand over his chest.

"Sorry, but we were on Mars," said Calico.

"You look worried. What's wrong?"

"We have a major development," said Calico, taking a seat in a red plastic chair shaped like a giant hand. Quotient floated above them, providing more light than the ambient light from the computer.

Calico quickly recapped her conversation with Oscar-Jen. Englehart leaned back in his director's chair, frowning, twiddling his thumbs. He listened intently, something Calico appreciated. Englehart was an exceptional listener. Most men didn't listen to anything. Englehart was a better listener than most women.

"I'm not sure what to make of this offer," said Calico as she concluded.

Englehart took off his hat, ran his hands through his hair, wiped his glasses on the tail of his shirt, and sighed. "Me either. This is most interesting."

"Or dangerous. I'm not sure which."

Englehart put his elbows on the desk and clasped his hands. Calico leaned forward as Englehart said, "Finding a ship isn't an issue, ironically."

"Of course not," said Calico, for they both knew the secret of Red Kelkirkstadt, it being built on an alien spacecraft.

"It's entirely possible Clegg *is* with us. It's entirely possible he's *not*. So, let's think about this a moment. If he's not, what would be his objective?" asked Englehart thoughtfully.

"Probably to figure out how to stop Quotient, who is, after all, the lynchpin to our plan," said Calico immediately.

"Then why come to you with a proposal that negates that?"

Calico cocked her head and frowned. "A valid point."

"If he is working for us, he must know the only way to make it work with Ops is non-lethal. I think he's sincere, but we could never trust him. He could slip a poison pill of some type into our plans somewhere. Do we truly need him?"

She frowned and her brow furrowed. "That is a good question. There are complications, so I'm not sure. Father abandoned the idea of alien spacecraft as the tachyonic influx source sometime around 2018. But I'm not sure entirely *why*. There was a lot going on back then with Hart dying and Kosar trying to lead an insurgence inside the Consortium with his COVID release. I also know the craft doesn't have a standard tachyon well, like the crafts found on Earth. Perhaps it was technical, but the problem is, technologically, it's not really my field."

"Nor mine. But that leaves us with this," and he leaned back, "either Clegg is smarter than any of the Consortium people your father worked with to figure this out, or it's a sham and a way to get access to you and Quotient or something inside the Consortium's inner circle."

"He is very smart," admitted Calico.

"Our liability now is your father's death. None of us had planned on that, and we don't know why he abandoned this line of thinking, or if he truly did."

"I've thought about that. We still centered Red Kelkirkstadt over the alien ship that landed there centuries ago. He must have thought at some point he might be able to use it for something — other than as a basic power source, of course."

"Who would he talk to about this?" asked Englehart after a moment's thought.

"My father kept his own counsel in terms of his personal plans, and when he had the rare moment of doubt, he consulted you or I. Or perhaps Sigurdsson, but given his mercurial nature, I don't want to talk to him about any of this."

Englehart nodded quickly. "Agreed."

"But in *scientific* terms, he'd talk to a wide range of people. He was quite willing to learn."

"Who would be the consortium's expert in this field?"

Calico frowned. "Probably Ainley, but he died last year, some type of car accident in Greece. After that . . . well, it would have to be Al Starlin."

"Jim's brother?"

"The same."

Englehart nodded. "Would Ainley have files we'd have access to?"

"Yes, but he was a pretentious and meticulous man. Reading through is files will take time. I'd assume Al could give us a reasonable synopsis in 20-30 minutes."

"Then let's go to him."

Calico pulled out her phone. "I'll call him first. I've found popping in on people like Al unexpectedly is not good for them."

It was now just after midnight in Al's suburban Chicago home on the west side of Winnetka. His home was a single-story, rectangular, 2,000-foot monolith that was brown brick with red trim and three bedrooms. But presently, Al lived alone with his dog, a retriever named Fetch, and a gray kitty named Kat.

Al wasn't good with names. A forty-two-year-old tall man, balding with a brown mustache, soft brown eyes, a congenial face, and a physique typical of a businessman — white, soft, a bit of a belly. He wore jeans and a short-sleeved shirt that white with black pinstripes. He wore thick-framed glasses. Sitting at his desk in a very messy bedroom that looked more appropriate for a teenager circa 1998, he wasn't wearing socks as he had the heat running full blast and the temperature in the home was eight-two degrees.

When the phone rang, he sneezed as he reached over and picked it up, cursing. "Hello?"

"It's Calico and Englehart. We have to talk."

Suddenly, Al was alert. "When?"

"We'll be there in five seconds."

"Fuck. Okay."

Al quickly put on some blue slippers, then walked into the kitchen. The kitchen was all stainless-steel appliances and black and white cabinets. There was little on the counters other than one big plastic jar of chocolate chip cookies and another of mini-sized Hershey bars. He took the last eight mini-Hershey bars and sat at the brown kitchen table.

Calico and Englehart, via Quotient, arrived.

"That *always* is freaky," said Al, running a hand through his hair.

"Sorry," said Calico. "But it is expedient."

The dining room table was small. Al pulled out a chair and said, "Have a seat. Sorry I'm not at my best. I was working on some research."

Calico sat across from Al, who had his back to the refrigerator, and Englehart sat to Calico's left, Al's right.

Al started eating the candy and said, "Not to be rude, but I've got a head cold and it's midnight, so I hope this is important."

"It is," said Calico. She quickly recapped, succinctly and efficiently.

When she finished, Al, who kept steadily eating the candy bars while listening, paused and nodded. "Wow. Quite a story. Clegg. Huh."

"We can research Ainley's work, but we assume you know it and can give us a quick synopsis to help us make a decision on what to do with Clegg," said Calico.

Al resumed eating. Between bites, he said, "Well, you can forget the alien ship idea. We gave that up in early '18, as I recall."

"That's roughly my recollection, but I was never involved in the details. Why did you abandon the theory?" asked Calico.

Al opened his last candy bar. "I'll only tell you if, after we're done, you go get more candy. When I'm sick, this shit is all that tastes good."

Calico smiled thinly. "Agreed."

"The problem is that you can't account for what Ainley terms Tachyonic Inverter Flux, or TIF. Take your alien spaceship," and he held up his right hand. "It's here. Say, downtown Tokyo." He held up his left hand. "When it opens a portal to shift through dimensions, for a moment in time it will exist both here and here," he said, shaking both hands.

"Agreed," said Englehart, nodding.

Al nodded. "Good. In that moment in time, you're getting Tachyonic Inverter Flux. Think of it as positive and negative coefficients on a graph. You exist in both spaces. Simultaneously. Now, this shouldn't be a problem if the ship is working right. I mean, if it wasn't able to be compensated for, you'd never get anywhere.

"The problem comes in if the TIF has a bounce-back event. Then your portal lets loose a surge of tachyons and anti-matter that is . . . beyond catastrophic. It would make the Earth look like an apple that someone took a big bite out of. Which, I guess is okay maybe if you're over the Pacific Ocean. But certainly not if you're over, say, Tokyo as I said before."

Calico nodded. "I can see the problem."

"Most aliens don't have this problem because they portal from outer space. But from what I understood from your father, there were no ships on Earth that had been found that were capable of getting *into* outer space at this point in time."

"As far as I know, true," said Calico. She rubbed her temples. "I can see why this would be abandoned. It wouldn't be worth the risk."

"Yes."

Englehart frowned and put out a questioning hand. "Then why did Kelkirk build the city over the ship buried under the surface of Mars?"

Al said, "To keep anyone else from finding it. There was never any intent to use it, once we determined this. And it's unlikely it's workable anyhow. We'd estimated that ship to be nearly two million years old."

"I have a '48 jeep that works just fine," said Englehart with a smile.

Al laughed. "This is a just a wee-tad older."

Calico said, "This has been most helpful. Basically, you see no way Clegg can help us on a practical level."

Quickly, Al shook his head. "No, you're reading into my words with *that*. I'm saying *Ainley and I* didn't see a way to do it that was safe. And Ainley did have some discussions with Staurvosky on this, but I don't know how far that went. You'd have to talk to him. Clegg has access to Ops resources and is brilliant in his own right. He may well have a way to do it. For all we know, Ops knows about the ship on Mars and might know things your father didn't. I wouldn't dismiss the ideal."

"I see," she said with a frown. Then she rose and said, "Al, I will visit the corner store and pick you up some candy bars if, while I am gone, you'll make some very black coffee. I have a long night ahead."

"Deal."

Calico turned to Englehart. "Let's walk to the garage."

The garage was an attached two-car garage, although Al had a 14-foot sailboat in one slot and his three-year-old Prius in the other. Calico and Englehart stepped down a step from the side door and into the garage, which had a large crack down the middle of the concrete and was exceptionally neat and organized.

Turning to Englehart, with Quotient floating over her, Calico said, "What are your thoughts?"

"My thoughts would be that it's worth pursuing, but we have to keep Clegg on Mars, isolated from Ops. At least for a day or two until we can assess Ainley's notes and perhaps talk to Staurvosky. I doubt he knows more than Al, however."

"I would agree," said Calico.

Englehart rubbed his chin. "My advice, and it is nothing more than that, dear, is to move slowly — but move. If Al thinks it's worth the risk, then it probably is worth the risk."

Calico smiled thinly and nodded. "I agree."

"Let's talk more tomorrow, but for now, I need to get back. That script starts shooting in the morning. I'm the last hope."

She smiled. "Quotient will return you."

"It's the last time I let a Canadian write for the show," he muttered.

She laughed. "Don't be a baby. I'll talk to you soon."

Quotient then vanished with Englehart.

A few seconds later, he returned. She said to him, "*(&(*&*(."

Quotient quivered.

Calico then exited the back door of the garage and walked through the yellow grass in the back yard towards a rear gate in the chain-link fence. She went through to an alley, then cut through a parking lot to the corner store, a local market situated next to a barber shop.

Once inside, she saw the cashier, a tall black man named Bobby. He looked at her with surprise. She wasn't typical of the local clientele. Right next to the register were giant-size Hershey bars on sale. She said, "I'll take six."

After she paid, he said, "Have a good night. Be careful."

"Sure. You too."

Then she walked back towards Al's house. The night was clear, the stars bright, and it was crisp but not cold.

In the parking lot, she suddenly began to feel a sense of being utterly overwhelmed. What the Hell was she doing? She held the fate of humanity in her hands, and that was a very heavy burden. She wanted to succeed because she wanted humanity to survive, obviously, but also to redeem her father's name and also to prove something for herself, that she was capable of being the type of leader he had been.

Her burden was heavy.

But she took a deep breath and pushed these thoughts aside. There was no time for introspection or self-pity at the moment.

Returning to Al's house with Quotient, she entered and tossed him the candy bars as she said, "You owe me ten dollars."

He sneezed, then laughed. "Consider it my fee for waking me up in the middle of the night and talk scientific research."

Calico had to laugh mildly at that. "An equal exchange. I agree to your terms. I will do some research on Ainley's notes. I may contact you again with questions."

Al looked at her. "All jokes aside, I'll be ready. I know how fucking important this is."

"Thanks."

"Good luck," said Al.

Calico then walked to the garage and vanished, leaving Al behind to eat one more chocolate bar before going to bed.

Chapter Ten
Coming to Terms
November 16, 2020

Yellow woke up in bed alone about an hour before Jen was due to meet Calico, at five American Eastern time. She wasn't sure where Smith was, then she remembered it was his rotation to watch Clegg-Saunders.

Restless, she got up and showered. Their bedroom had a large, single bed covered with blue and white bedspread and sheets, and most of two walls were obscured by a pair of giant aquariums with five dozen fish. The other wall was mostly a screen and a small bookcase with a few texts. The bathroom was functional, painted yellow with black trim. After showering, she put on black dress pants and a yellow turtleneck sweater with a white collared shirt under it.

Once she had coffee, she texted Calico for a status and received an immediate response.

LIBRARY

Yellow nodded to herself and found a small scooter, a two-wheeled device that southern Californians used on the beach boardwalk to get around. It had a maximum speed of about 30 kilometers per hour. She used it to get to the library, which was really just a modest hall in the government building. Calico was alone in the library, for it was closed, but she had total access to everything. She was working on a computer terminal, one of six set up in the divide between the reception desk and the back storerooms.

"You're up early," said Yellow.

"On the contrary, I am up late. I've been working since I got back from Earth a few hours ago."

"Anything of value?"

She nodded and leaned back, folding her arms over her chest. "Yes. We're going to allow Clegg to do some research, but he's staying here. I'll take him-her for a tour, show the basics of the city, but I have to deal with the work of the general population today."

"Trouble?" asked Yellow, arching an eyebrow.

"Nothing unexpected, but I'm essentially mayor now." She made a face. "Not a position I covet or desire, but critical at this particular point in time."

"I understand," she said sympathetically.

"I need you and Smith to stay here and watch every move she makes. Given what all happened in Portland and San Diego, you two are much safer here anyhow."

"We can do that, but we're not knowledgeable on her work. What are we watching for?"

"I'm not giving him-her access to anything critical yet. Based on Ainley's notes, what Clegg proposes is feasible but there are an awful lot of critical conditions. I do not believe it is practical, just theoretically possible. Giving Clegg a chance won't hurt anything; if he succeeds, wonderful, but if not, nothing is lost. We just have to make sure this isn't some type of trick to harm me or Quotient."

"Sure," said Yellow nervously.

"I'm also going to go find Staurvosky and see if he can shed any light. I rarely dealt with him personally, perhaps a couple of times. He did most of his work directly with my father."

"That's fine. Smith and I can handle things here. We'll give Clegg an official lab?"

"Yes. All that basic set up. I'll talk to him and set everything up before I go."

"Thanks."

With that, Calico rose and said, "In fact, I should do that now. It's a little early local time, but that won't matter. I'll check with you before I go."

"Sure."

"How are the animals?"

Yellow's face lit up. "Doing great! I'm very pleased."

"Good. Stay alert."

"Of course. Good luck."

Calico left Yellow behind and scooted using another scooter to Clegg's building.

"Are you sure this will work, Oscar? Now that we're here, I'm scared," said Jen from inside the head, as Oscar was in charge of the body.

"I don't know if it will or not, but I think it's our best hope."

"I'll take care of us, Jen," said Anissa confidently.

Jen nodded. "Cara is angry. I can feel it."

Anissa laughed. "She's always angry! That's what she does!"

Suddenly, there was a knock on the door. Calico. Oscar-Jen opened the door wearing a brown sweatshirt and loose-fitting jeans, no shoes or socks.

"You're early," said Oscar.

"I am sorry, but things have come up. May we speak for a moment?"

"Sure. Come in."

Calico stepped inside. "I'm willing to work with you."

"Good. I'm pleased to work with you," said Oscar-Jen.

Calico cocked her head. It was odd watching Saunders, a passive, soft woman, move aggressively and assertively like a man, jutting her chest and chin out. The distinctive body language was something Calico looked for.

"I'd like to outline the city, then show you to the lab facilities."

"That's splendid," said Oscar-Jen. "Right now?"

"Yes. You should have a scooter here in the room, in the main closet," said Calico, pointing to a door near the bathroom.

"Ah, yes," said Oscar-Jen. The scooter was a simply two-wheeled scooter with a control and an emergency brake. There was a ten-inch screen on it and a few dials.

As Jen exited the room, it locked automatically. All the locks were bio-locks. She looked at the scooter and said, "Helmet?"

"The scooter is auto-speed controlled and will drive itself. Maximum speed is ten miles per hour. The inside buildings have padded floors, and we won't be going spelunking, so you should be fine, explained Calico.

"Certainly."

She pointed at the video screen, tapped a button, and a map appeared. "This will guide you. The scooters are all bio-controlled, linked to authorize you based on aura and eye-scans. They won't go where you are not allowed to go."

"Fortuitous."

"Damn machines!" said Anissa-internally.

Oscar-Jen ignored her and added, "My, this is a large place."

"I'll explain as we ride to the research facilities. They're down Hilderbrand Strasse."

They exited the building onto a corridor that looked like a brick road, but it was in fact a unique organic pavement mix perfectly designed for the wheels of the scooter.

As they rode, Jen noticed a few people walking and on scooters. "How many people are here?"

"Several thousand."

"This is the main part of the city?"

Calico was leading, so she was slightly ahead, but close enough to talk. The motors of the scooters were virtually silent and didn't impede their conversation. She said, "The main city is a cylinder-shaped hub in the center of town. The government building is the central object. The living facilities ring it. Then there's an outer layer of various maintenance facilities, and then the fourth layer is the domes which seal us off from outer space."

"And if they fail?"

Calico didn't take offense. It was a practical question. "There are three layers of domes working on separate systems. Same with the fields underground. They are a unique tachyon and anti-matter positive force, so at a certain point once they exist they grow and self-sustain themselves."

"What the ding-dong is she talking about?" asked Anissa internally.

Jen just said, "We'll explain later."

"Yeah, whatever," said Anissa. She hated it when they were talking about scientific things she didn't understand. She had been a trauma nurse. She was accomplished more than her belief in herself. But Clegg and Saunders were ground-breaking scientists. They were out of anyone's league many times, even their own peers.

"The majority of Red Kelkirkstadt is actually underground, inside the crater," said Calico, and they turned left at an intersection with a four-way stop. "This is the only city with inhabitants. We have others under construction."

"Amazing."

"Thank you."

The buildings in this area were all single-story like warehouses. There was little color. They were composed of some type of pre-fab construction, like the temporary trailers FEMA used after hurricanes and tornadoes for emergency housing.

"Here's a station."

They came to what looked like a freestanding elevator outside one of the buildings. There were three stations. Each had a control panel. There was a scooter docking station to the left. Calico docked her scooter, so Jen did the same. Then they stepped into the elevator. The numbers, listed in German and English, went to forty-seven.

"That represents stories?" asked Jen as they began to descend.

"We call them layers here, but it's a rough equivalent, yes."

Oscar-Jen nodded. Internally, Jen felt queasy, not thrilled with being trapped underground. Inevitably, the memory of the slaughter at the complex in 2004 seeped into her memory.

How different would her life be if that day never happened?

At the bottom, the doors automatically opened into the lobby of a building. It looked like an elevator lobby in a hospital, complete with a plastic plant and guide board.

"Your lab is three," said Calico, leading Oscar-Jen to the left.

Once there, they entered. The lab was a perfectly acceptable medical research lab and had several paranormal devices as well, including aural detectors, tachyon surge readers, and anti-matter alert devices. The room had six long tables, each covered with equipment, and was surrounded by cases full of drugs and tablets, all locked. About 1,0000 square feet, It also had a stainless-steel refrigerator, sink, and a tiny cutout from cheap drywall for a private bathroom. The far wall was a landscape painting of the Martian surface with a violet sky due to clouds in the distance.

"It will be fine, thank you," said Oscar-Jen.

"The cafeteria is six, which is down the hall. You have access to that. You can also go back to the surface and use your scooter, but if you try to wander, the alarms will sound. We have to be very careful about access here. Everyone is new. People get lost."

"Yeah, right," said Anissa internally.

"I understand," said Oscar-Jen.

He and Calico looked at each other for a moment, each knowing the reality, and the moment passed. Then Oscar-Jen asked, "How did you build such a place before Quotient?"

Calico smiled. "That's a long story for a better time."

"Very well. I'll get to work. Where will you be?"

"I have tedious government affairs to handle today. We can discuss details of the research when I return. I have the works of Ainley. You know of him?"

"Of course. Those are valuable."

Calico didn't know about that, but she didn't react. "We'll review those and such. Let's say over dinner?" Then she made a face. "Today might get odd. If not, then tomorrow?"

"Whatever fits your needs."

"Good." She put out her hand, and they shook as Calico added, "Thank you for seeking to save the world."

"It's my pleasure, but I'd like to work out a bit and get breakfast before I start, get the old blood pumping."

"There is a small gym, it's in eight. Yellow and Smith are here for all of your needs. Just dial 112 on the phone."

Calico started to exit, but paused and snapped her fingers. "Oh, uh, one more thing. Doctor Trixie Taylor is here. I know she and Ops are, ah, not on good terms."

"That's putting it *mildly*," said Oscar-Jen.

"There are circumstances around Trixie Ops does not understand. Be warned, do not harm her or there will be repercussions."

"Understood — assuming, of course, *she* has the same understanding."

"She does and thank you. Enjoy."

"I shall. Breakfast and a workout are good for the mind."

Chapter Eleven
The Rabble
November 16, 2020

"Doughnuts are not a breakfast," said Calico to Englehart as she entered their private quarters in the main government building, which was the top level of the inner spire, which had a disturbing resemblance to Seattle's Space Needle.

"They are for us Hollywood types," he said with a weary smile.

He rose from his desk to hug her, having been portaled in by Quotient about thirty minutes earlier, just after finishing the emergency script. He was now reviewing some non-essential contracts on his computer, mostly killing time while waiting for Calico. In the background, Diana Ross sung at a very low volume. The windows overlooked the city, genuine windows, a stunning image of buildings mixed with rock and an orange hued sky. He had changed and was wearing a blue and white Hawaiian shirt, straw hat, white shorts and no shoes or socks, he clearly was in writing mode. The box of a dozen doughnuts, which Quotient portaled with the, sat on his desk. It was the same pink box that seemed universal for doughnuts and was half-empty.

"Which is why you die young. Eat a banana," chided Calico.

He made a face and hugged her. "You only get on me about diet when you feel insecure. Let's talk."

They sat on a large, zebra-striped sectional that faced a wall unit television, which was broadcasting the local news. Calico folded her legs up under her. Englehart sat on her right, leaning his head on his arm, which was on the end of the sectional. A glass coffee table offset the otherwise generic tenor of the room, which was decorated in navy blue and white. This room was mostly for Englehart to work, so it was set up to be conducive to writing, and most of the effort had therefore gone into the sound system and not the décor.

"I'm just agitated about the situation with the general population. With Saunders being here, they are a complication I don't need. Complications are for your stupid stories, not my plan," she muttered.

"Well, stay calm. The general population isn't behaving differently than predicted. We've had a 2.3 percent suicide rate, which is less than the 2.8 percent prediction, and we've had to jail six people, which is exactly on the prediction."

"Annoyances, nonetheless."

He studied her. There were circles under her eyes and she was clearly agitated. "You're not sleeping well, and as challenging as building a new world can be, you've relished the task. Something else is bothering you, and its best we talk and get it out."

She gave a half-smile and looked at him. "You know me well, my friend. In many ways you are more a father than Father was."

"I am honored by your feelings, but you are more a daughter to me than my own child would have been . . . or could have been," he said, for just a moment feeling tingle of pain at the loss of his wife, Piper, and son, Joey, so many years ago. Their murder was an event Calico had helped him avenge. Quickly shaking it off, he said, "How do you feel about all of this?"

"I feel overwhelmed at times. But . . . I feel . . . this will surprise you."

"Oh?"

She turned to look at him directly, as if about to confess to a priest. "I feel dirty, dear Englehart. Dirty. Sullied."

"For Portland?"

Quickly, she shook her head. "Oh, no. I feel regret over that, but not guilt. We knew deaths of innocents were inevitable. I long ago passed that. No . . . it's Ray."

Englehart was surprised. "Ray?"

Looking away, she then spoke without looking at him. "I . . . when he had the idea of using lunar light to enhance his channeling, that he could not be allowed to survive . . . I feel dirty that I had sex with him. I used him, which I have done with others, but only for my own pleasure. Not in such a manipulative fashion."

And then she had a tear, and wiped it out as she added, "I really *liked* him, Englehart. He was a friend, not just a partner. He was somewhat limited in his thinking, but a good man nonetheless. His death was inevitable. The spell could not have worked without it. Killing him . . . hurt me."

Englehart said gently, "I know. I have the same feelings . . . is the pain about killing him or using him?"

"Both, I feel . . . no, that's not quite right," she said, in obvious pain. "I . . . got too close by sleeping with him. Killing him was . . . that was inevitable. He would have died painfully in the spell anyhow, and he knew he would die in this event. Killing him was a mercy, to spare him further pain."

"So was sleeping with him," said Englehart.

"I suppose," she said, clearly not in agreement.

He paused. He thought there was a deeper issue, but he also knew Calico *rarely* engaged in sex after her lover, Keith, was killed by the Society in 2013. Having sex with Ray, who almost immediately afterward was killed . . . even though everyone knew it would happen, Englehart knew this act could definitely send Calico's subconscious gymnastics tumbling.

Carefully, he said, "They're valid feelings. He was a good man. He gave his life for our cause . . . and for what it's worth, I'm sure his last night was one of the best of his life thanks to your charity. Do you want to talk about it?"

She looked at him. "I have not used myself in . . . in *that* fashion before. It was purely to control him, keep him from thinking about trying to execute the ritual without dying. I . . . that was why I had Karla arrange to skewer him, not just because it's a quicker death . . . than psychic heat burn. I . . . I am not a cold person. I have feelings."

"Of course."

She shook her head sadly. "You know, I had a very sheltered sex life until I met Keith. Certainly, I was not a virgin. But my sexual encounters were with Society members arranged or at least prodded by my father and his contacts. I was a virgin until I as eighteen and had only a handful of encounters until I met Keith. And after . . . after his . . . death . . . I've been mostly celibate. I don't have time for it."

Englehart nodded, realizing this was a significant emotional moment for Calico, and one she had to work through on her own. "I can't assuage your feelings, Calico. Your feelings are what they are. We have all done things in this endeavor that we regret and that have caused us pain and have challenged us. You must remember the joy you brought him in the moment, and that he made all of this possible without causing many, many more deaths. It's the only way to cope."

She forced a smile and a nod and said, "I know that. But it hurts."

"Pain is okay."

She nodded. "I feel like I'm being a child. With all that's going on, I'm moping about a one-night stand."

"No, don't say that," said Englehart, "for your compassion and feelings are what has driven this project. You need them. And they make you who you are, the woman we all need and love. Just feel the pain and allow it to pass through."

She rose. "I . . . I will. I always like to talk to you. You are a very kind man."

"I'm just a good listener." He chuckled. "Besides, every conversation for a writer is fodder for a future episode."

"I will claim royalties." She sighed. "To business, my friend. I need to do some research earthside."

"There is an agenda item first," said Englehart, rising as well. "Kurt called. The Pillow couple was found in an unauthorized section."

Her eyes narrowed. "What?"

"They're in cell block B."

"I'll be there directly. Call Kurt."

"They were on the central line for the power plant," said Kurt Drunkenmiller, Calico's lead Police Chief for Red Kelkirkstadt.

"How?" she asked.

"That's what I want to know."

Kurt was a tall, thin man who was gaunt and looked a bit like a vampire that woke up on the wrong side of the bed. He had curly black hair and brown eyes, and always looked about to bite someone. His tone of voice was always even and level, and he had been with the Kelkirk family as an operative since 2008, when Calico's father brought him in from Bonn for an assignment.

"Let's go," said Calico. She had changed into a black blouse with red dots, a black leather jacket, and gray slacks with black heels. She looked striking and pissed off.

They entered the main jail and proceeded to cell block B, which had two rooms. In room A were the Pillow couple. They were in cells that were narrow and only allowed them to stand, which they had been doing for quite some time.

Calico said to Kurt, "I'll talk to them."

"As you wish."

Calico entered. The Pillows were each in their mid-sixties, a pair of genetic research scientists trying to cure birth defects. They owned labs in New York and Florida, and they primarily had been working out of Tampa Bay for the last decade as Judy had significant rheumatoid arthritis. She was round and chubby with white hair like Mrs. Santa Claus, while he was tall, thin, and bald with glasses and looked like a school principal.

Calico stood before them. "I am Calico Kelkirk. I am the founder and leader of this city. The rules were clearly outlined to you. How did you violate the authorization zone?"

They said nothing.

Calico approached Jack. "Sir . . . do not be tedious. I assure you, I have no qualms about torturing you just because you are old. I will make your wife suffer and you will tell me. Spare her the pain. Take your punishment, talk to me, and you can rejoin our society."

"We . . . we didn't. We just were out for a walk, I swear."

Cocking her head, Calico studied him. She had an app on her watch that served as a truth detector by measuring heartrate.

When she checked it, she was surprised to find he was telling the truth. But like an expert poker player, she didn't show it. Instead, she said to Judi, "Is that the case?"

"Yes. Please, standing on this concrete, it hurts."

"I will speak to the Chief."

She exited and said to Kurt, "They speak the truth. Release them but confine them to quarters. We have to figure out what caused the security to fail."

Kurt looked alarmed. "You're certain it failed?"

"No, but reasonably confident it did, which is a significant breach. Have there been any other incidents?"

"The only oddity in the last forty-eight hours was a power loss in Bleeker building. We think it was a rat."

Calico arched an eyebrow. "A rat? We don't have rats."

"We have people and garbage, ma'am, so we have rats. Anyhow, the cable was chewed."

Calico's eyes narrowed and she frowned. "Send me the details. I'll be in my quarters."

"Of course."

Storming back to her quarters, Calico processed this information. It was a surprise, and surprises were dangerous.

Chapter Twelve
Trixie vs. Jen
November 16, 2020

"Mind your own business," snapped Trixie at the guard at the front of the building as she entered at 8:03, a couple of hours after Jen and Calico had their meeting. The guard had merely asked her how she was feeling. He took that to mean it was that time of the month.

Trixie was terrified, of course. But she was committed, and she frankly just wanted to get the task completed and resume what had become her normal life. She was worried about the consequences from Calico, but that was nothing compared to her fear of the island in Hell.

Nothing.

Meanwhile, Jennifer liked working out in the morning. Well, that wasn't technically true . . . on many levels. First, Jennifer didn't like working out at all. Nor did Anissa. Clegg liked it, and Jennifer's alter Donnie, the sulky teenager, liked playing basketball. Second, there wasn't any real morning on Mars. Everything in Red Kelkirkstadt was derived to maintain a similar Earth environment to help with the transition.

Her alter Donnie, the sullen teenage boy, was shooting hoops in the back corner of the gym near the entry to the locker rooms. The middle of the gym was separated by a volleyball net. The opposite side from Donnie had an area for lifting weights. There were a variety of volleyballs, soccer balls, and basketballs sitting around. There were bleachers on the long sides, all empty of course. The gym itself was off limits to the general population. But per Calico's orders, administration had given Jen access. Trixie, of course, had full access to nearly every facility in Red Kelkirkstadt.

Since Jen's integration nearly fifteen years ago, her normal pattern had been to try and give the alters what they needed when possible. Having free access to a gym was normal on the parallel world, so this was a routine Jen had started after being sealed off there in 2016.

Donnie was having great fun, moving around imaginary picks set at the corners of the multi-colored lines and taking pull up jumpers. While Donnie worked out, in charge of the body though he didn't really know it, Oscar cleared his mind. It was quiet, and for once everyone else was leaving him alone and letting him have fun.

Then the lights went out.

Instantly, Jen was back in charge as Donnie retreated and Jen, sensing it, resumed control of her body.

The switch was almost seamless, but Jen lost control of the dribble and the ball bounced into the bleachers. Just as Jen crouched into a defensive position and turned to check the doors, a light came on. But of the eight large, circular overhead lights, only the one in this corner of the gym turned on.

Then she heard clapping.

Wary, Jen turned towards the sound of the clapping, which was the doorway at the far end of the gym. Then the small light that lit the two side walls leading to the door under the bleachers turned on, and Jen realized who was there.

Trixie Taylor.

Taylor wore olive-green leggings, black and white heels, and a white blouse that buttoned down the middle. The buttons were undone in a manner to show some cleavage. She also wore a gold necklace that plunged into her cleavage and an expensive gold watch. Her hair and make-up were impeccable, though much of her physical appearance was a glamour to reduce her age and heighten her better features. Underneath, she was an ugly duckling. And given her clothes, she obviously wasn't at the gym to work out.

"Very amusing, Saunders. Trying to turn pro?" Trixie was being bold, covering her own intense fear. She wasn't sure she could take Saunders and was even more afraid of what Julie would do if Saunders won. Trixie wasn't just fighting for her life but for her soul.

It was a tad stressful.

"Be alert," said Oscar in Jen's mind.

"For once, you didn't have to tell me. I don't trust her further than Anissa could throw her," said Jen internally.

"Hey! Well, okay. I feel the same. Let's just say we don't trust her further than Dr. Grump could throw her," said Anissa.

Trixie had an object in her hand that looked like a cell phone, but it wasn't. Jen wasn't certain what it was. Trixie stepped forward and the lights behind her turned off, but the circle where she was standing, which was the corner opposite Jen, turned on.

"Did you need something?" asked Jen. She was warily scanning for an ambush, but the gym seemed empty other than the two of them.

"I need a lot of things," said Trixie with a coy smile. "You know much about me, Saunders?"

At this moment, Clegg took over the control of the body. "What I've read from the reports of Meredith Patience . . . you *sicken* me, to be honest. If you weren't under Calico's protection, I'd have you put away."

Trixie made a face to pretend she was thinking it over, then she laughed. She was slowly walking along the far, red line, moving towards Jen but on the opposite side of the gym. "Fair enough. I prefer to think I'm an artist."

"Artist? You're a serial killer . . . at best."

Looking offended, Trixie stopped walking and shook her head. "No, I'm nothing like that. I don't kill to kill, Saunders. I'm a doctor. I'm a real doctor, by the way. When I was a child in Tampa, I learned of the power a TM can gain . . . and medical torture is extraordinary. It's perfectly legal in most cases. Hospitals are . . . wonderful places."

She resumed walking.

Retaking control, Jen said, "You're sick."

"She's depraved," said Oscar internally.

Jen was surprised. It was rare Oscar emoted such disgust or anger towards anything, but Taylor really pushed his buttons. Perhaps it was that she reminded him of himself during the war, when the Nazis forced him to perform medical experiments on his own people, something Jen did not know. Her alter Cara, the one holding Jen's anger, knew but was keeping it secret. That, combined with the fact to maintain the undercover role meant Jen had to put up with Taylor, was making him emotional.

Anissa sensed it and chided internally, "Be cool, Oscar. Jen needs our help."

Jen threw Trixie the basketball. "Do you want to play?"

"I am playing," said Trixie with a wicked, predatory smile. "Do you know what my thing was back in LA, back before blondie fucked up our little club?"

"Medical torture. Medical experiments."

Trixie held up a hand and paused her walk again. She was now directly opposite Jen. Both women were scanning the environment rapidly. Trixie said, "No. I was known for being unique. Yes, my form of art was medical torture. But I never repeated a torture. I always found a new way to inflict painful death on a human body. Now . . . as amazing as it might seem, the ways to inflict pain on a human are almost infinite. But there's one area I've never explored."

"That being psychotherapy, obviously," said Oscar, making a dry and unfunny joke that Jen didn't repeat.

"We know Clegg exists inside you. I don't know if there are others in your fucked up little head, but I bet there are. Multiple personalities are fascinating. I can inflict the same pain on you when different personalities are in charge and get a completely different reaction, at least in theory. I would love to try that on you, because you see, I think you're a lying sham. You're here for Ops, no matter what you say or what Calico thinks. And I'm not having you ruin what is the best thing to ever happen to me or to Earth."

"I'm under Calico's protection. If I disappear into your basement, she'll know."

"Maybe," said Trixie, again appearing to think it over. "So maybe it's better just to kill your fucking ass right now."

Then she attacked. She used TK to drop the ropes from the rafters, sending them after Jen like snakes, while simultaneously hurling ten-pound weights from a weight rack in the corner at Jen's head.

But Jen wasn't fighting. Instantly, Anissa took over the shared physical body. During the time Jen was comatose and Oscar retreated with her to try and integrate her multiple personalities and heal her, Anissa had been the person in charge of Jen's body. For over a year, *she* had been Jennifer Saunders, leading of the resistance in the parallel world. Anissa understood fighting. She didn't necessarily like it, but she could do it.

Trixie was not a good combatant. She usually used subterfuge, usually her feminine wiles, to deceive and subjugate her victims. Fear of the Four Cornered Wheel was all that was driving her to this fight, and she knew she had to win fast. If the battle was long, either Jennifer would win, or Yellow and Smith would break it up.

Anissa was adroit enough to handle the weights in the obvious manner. She simply ducked and rolled forward, doing a summersault while they dialed over her head and embedded themselves in the drywall. The ropes were after her, however, and one snagged her right ankle.

Trixie quickly attacked, using TK to hurl the volleyball net to tangle her opponent, but Anissa was ready. She grabbed it and flung it back at Trixie, who ducked allowing the net to fall to the floor. Anissa simultaneously hurled a basketball into the fire alarm. The impact was enough to set off the alarm, which had two immediate consequences.

First, the sprinklers activated, soaking the gym in a downpour.

Second, Yellow and Smith were alerted. Smith was in the bathroom, but Yellow was at the check-in desk just yards away.

Trixie knew she had only seconds. She pulled the rope that had looped around Jen's ankle and flung her into the bleachers, while simultaneously hurling an empty weight bar at her like a javelin.

Anissa was able to stave off the bar by hurling the basketball into its path, deflecting its course.

At that moment, Yellow raced in. "Stop!"

But the second Yellow paused in the door's entryway, Trixie summoned a huge wind to blow Yellow back outside the gym. Mixed with the water from the sprinklers, the wind hit Yellow like a piledriver and pushed her like a battering ram across the lobby, slamming her into the drywall under a bulletin board. She wasn't quite knocked out, but she was a bit loopy and had bruised two ribs. As a result, she stayed down, groaning.

Smith heard the impact of Yellow into the drywall. The bathrooms were next to the lobby. He literally leapt off the toilet and shoved himself into his pants. Racing outside, he saw Yellow first.

"Yellow! Yellow!"

Inside, Trixie knew she had only seconds to finish off her opponent. She put everything into one last maneuver, taking the wind that had struck Yellow and whipping it back towards her and then out, almost like a water whip.

Trixie's entire focus was on her attack, leaving her nothing for defense. Not an experienced combatant, she figured in the second it would take to strike with the water-whip, that was more than enough time.

It wasn't.

Anissa fired an empty bar via TK straight at Trixie's shins. The impact was as if a home-run hitter in the World Series had swung his bat right into Trixie's shins. This took less than a second.

"YEWARRRRRRRRRRGHHHHHHHHHH!" screamed Trixie as she pitched forward, both shins broken by the impact. She lost all control over the water-whip, and it dissolved into basically a hard rain shower.

Outside, Smith saw Yellow was semi-conscious. Hearing the combat, he raced into the doorway to find Trixie on the ground howling and Saunders racing towards Trixie.

"You did it!" shouted Jen internally to her friend.

Smith also raced to Trixie, who was bleeding significantly. But she was trying to use a healing spell as Smith approached.

Suddenly, Calico arrived. She had been alerted when Yellow's aural detector spiked, then used Quotient to immediately portal to the gym.

Quotient hovered ominously above her.

"*What is going on here?*" she shouted at the three people in the gym.

With a look of anguish, Trixie pointed at Saunders. "She started it."

"I did not! She did!" shouted Anissa through Jen.

"This battle is over!" shouted Calico. She looked at Smith. "Where is Yellow?"

He pointed to the lobby. "Out there. I was in the can. She got knocked into the lobby wall."

"Check on her. I'll handle this," said Calico with a glare that could have melted the sun.

Trixie continued to use her healing spell. The bleeding stopped, and gradually her legs returned to normal. She screamed the entire time, for the healing spell worked, but it did nothing to combat pain.

"Shut up, you baby," said Calico.

Trixie gave her a look to kill but said nothing. Tears rolled down her face.

Calico turned to Saunders. "Please sit on the bleachers."

Anissa sat and said, "Jen, I think I'd better let Oscar take control again. He's the one Calico related to."

"Agreed," said Jen internally.

"I shall assume command," said Clegg pleasantly.

Meanwhile, Calico looked up and said to Quotient, "*(&&(*^*&. ?? (*&(*&**..)"

"What did you tell him?" asked Oscar-Jen.

Calico said firmly, "To stop any aggressive action between you and Trixie."

"Thank you."

Trixie said again and very sullenly, "She started it."

Wearily, Calico said, "Can you stand yet? You are not very good at this."

Again, Trixie shot Calico a look that could have killed. "I'm getting up now. Thanks for your concern."

Calico snapped and pointed at Trixie. "*You* started this. I can tell by the battle pattern. Saunders is my guest! You are to guard her, not try and kill her!"

"I didn't try and kill her, just make her understand her place," snapped Trixie.

Calico slapped her. "Do *not* insult my intelligence. This was not sparring. You are confined to quarters for the time being. If you leave, Quotient will take action. *Permanent* action! *Is that understood*?" she asked, pronouncing each word of the last sentence slowly and firmly.

"Yes . . . yes," said Trixie with real fear. Suddenly, it occurred to her there could be worse things than Hell.

"Get out of my sight."

Trixie quickly stumbled away to her room, soaking wet.

As she exited the door, she passed Smith, who was helping a clearly groggy Yellow into the gym.

Yellow had a cut on her face and the back of her right hand, and she was clearly favoring her right side.

"Is she okay?" asked Calico worriedly.

"I'm fine," answered Yellow for herself. "Just some ribs. They broke or bruised or something. I healed them . . . I'm a little confused."

"Smith, make sure Trixie goes to her room," said Calico.

"Sure."

After he exited, Calico sat Yellow on the bleachers next to the door and asked, "What happened?"

"I heard the fire alarm. I was in the lobby answering a page. Smith was taking a crap . . . I raced in and that's the last I remember. I woke up kissing the wall."

"Trixie used wind to hurl her across the lobby into the wall," said Oscar-Jen.

Calico looked at her, nodded, then turned back to Yellow. "I'm sorry. Trixie is confined to quarters. Can you get Mr. Clegg or Miss Saunders, however she is to be addressed, back to quarters?"

"I can find my own way. She should see a doctor," said Oscar-Jen.

"Very well, thank you," said Calico. "I'd like a meeting. Is an hour okay?"

"That's fine."

"I'll call your room. Thank you. I apologize for Trixie. She will be punished."

"It's okay. If you work with the Devil, you *are* the Devil," said Oscar, and then he exited.

"Nice parting shot," said Jen internally to him.

"Thank you. I liked it as well."

Once they were gone, Calico said to Yellow, "Will you be okay?"

"I'm fine. Actually, I'm a little embarrassed. I walked right into that one. I just . . . didn't expect this."

Frowning, Calico said darkly, "Neither did I, which means something else is going on. I have work to do. Check in with me each hour on the hour."

Concerned, Yellow said, "Okay. Why are you so worried?"

"When people act in an abnormal manner, there's something motivating you that you don't know about. So what is driving Trixie?"

"You sure fucked that up," said Julie with a wry smirk as Trixie entered her room.

Soaking wet, her hair matted to her face, and dried blood staining her boots and legs, Trixie said, "I *will* kill that bitch now. Not for you. But for *this*. How dare she?"

Julie snorted. "You were trying to kill her, doctor."

"Fuck her. Asshole bitch. I'll rip her lungs out."

Julie chuckled. "I doubt it. She polished you off like a child. But it doesn't matter. Everything is now in place. Saunders is a threat, but not an insurmountable one, and I dare not risk you being exposed or injured trying to kill her again. So we make our move now."

"Now?" asked Trixie meekly.

Glaring with a dark smile, Julie said, "Unless you'd prefer to just be delivered to Hell?"

Quickly shaking her head, Trixie said, "No, no, no. We can move now."

Julie patted Trixie's cheek. Seductively, she said, "You're an excellent servant. You know . . . I can do more than spare you Hell. When the Great Escape begins, I will make you immortal. You will *never* have to face your victims."

Trixie's eyes widened. "You . . . you can do that?"

"Yes. I will reward your servitude, doctor." Then she turned cold. "But only if we succeed. And we need to move."

"Okay. Okay. Can I change clothes and dry off?"

"If you must," said Julie. "I will return. I need a few minutes on Earth for preparation."

But before Trixie could do or ask anything, the doorbell rang. Trixie checked the door. It was Calico. Trixie turned to ask Julie what to do, but Julie had vanished, so Trixie took that as an indication that it was necessary to speak with Calico.

"Hi," said Trixie as she opened the door.

"You're soaking wet. We need to talk," snapped Calico.

"Give me a minute to dry off and change clothes."

Calico stepped into the room. Once in the room, she paused, feeling an odd tingle. She ran an aural detection spell, which returned nothing.

Trixie took only three minutes to towel down and put on some spare clothes that were in the dirty laundry hamper in the bathroom but weren't really that dirty. She didn't wear any underwear. She had gray workout shorts and a black T-shirt with a spinning wheel that said, "Thinking." No socks.

Calico stood near the bed, arms folded over her chest, her legs pointed out in a defiant stance. "Your behavior today was unacceptable."

"I'm sorry," said Trixie. "I just . . . lost my head."

"No, you did not. You deliberately attacked her. Why?"

Trixie had no doubt the Four Cornered Wheel would leave her twisting in the wind if necessary and had no doubt if Calico suspected subterfuge that Calico would turn on her as well. She had to be bold with her defense.

Pointing and shoving her finger into Calico's chest, she snapped, "I'm defending *you*! Defending us! You *can't* trust a man like Clegg and a woman like Saunders! Multiple personalities aren't stable! She could have others in her head that might take over, ones we don't know about!"

Calico calmly removed Trixie's hand and said, "That is not *your* decision. You will remain confined to the administration building. Any more aggressive action towards Saunders, and I mean even a nasty look, and you will be . . . removed."

Their eyes met.

Then Trixie cracked. Trixie gave her a look, starting to shake. "I won't . . . don't do that."

"The decision is yours. I've made your options quite clear. Now, I have work to do. I will be on Earth a short time. Yellow and Smith are in in charge."

"Fine," said Trixie.

Calico exited. As she materialized in her office, which was rather sterile other than a holographic scene of the German forest covered in snow that wrapped around the walls, she found Yellow waiting.

"How did it go?" asked Yellow anxiously.

"There shouldn't be any more problems," said Calico firmly.

"What is next?"

"I need to find Staurvosky and delve into his research. You and Smith are in charge here. Trixie is confined to the admin buildings. Keep an eye on her. I have put cameras in her room. If she has contact with anyone, let me know."

"Of course. Will you be long?"

"I wouldn't expect so. A few hours, perhaps. Good luck."

"And you."

Once she was gone, Yellow called Smith, who was in the lobby of the condo building which Trixie occupied, just to see if she left. After Yellow recapped, Smith said, "We're guard dogs."

"For the moment. I'm checking the cameras. I don't see anyone with her. She's just sitting on the bed."

"Don't just sit there, dear. There's work to be done."

Julie stood before Trixie, who was sitting on the edge of her bed, shaking her head. Long ago, the four Cornered Wheel had learned to obscure her presence from cameras. She could make herself visible when she wanted to, and screen when she wanted to. Right now, she was screened.

Trixie looked up at her tormentor. "Like what? You heard Calico. If I leave, I wind up dead. I'm not losing my soul. I'd rather go to Hell."

Putting on a sexy, mock pout, Julie said, "I have some work to do on Earth. You need to be prepared to move when I get back. We will move fast, too fast for Calico to make a difference. The time for the Great Escape has arrived."

Trixie rolled her eyes. "You're the most melodramatic ghost I've ever met."

"I'm *not* a ghost," said Julie with a dark smile. "And soon all of your meat-bag friends will know it. I'll be back in just minutes. Get your ass off the bed and get ready."

Then she was gone.

In Berlin, it was late afternoon.

"Akkkkkkkkk! Give an old man some warning!" exclaimed German TM Julian Hahn as he ate a muffin in the penthouse of an insurance company office in Berlin. He was fifty-six with gray hair, a chubby face, and an arrogant air. Tall at six-two, he was a little overweight but in reasonable shape for his eyes. His eyes were a dark brown and he had big ears. He wore a gray suit with a white dress shirt and black and white striped tie, in full business mode.

Julie stepped forward and snapped, "The time is now. Trixie is in place. Calico is on Earth with Quotient but alert to return at a moment's notice."

Julian instantly pressed the intercom and sent an alert to Hickory, Sasha, and Bundt. The two women were Julian's acolytes, both twenty-four and had been found by Julian during one of his Consortium meetings in Prague. They looked very similar. Hickory had long, brown hair parted in the middle and very straight with blue eyes and a narrow face and frame. Sasha was much the same, but she had red highlights in her hair, wider eyes, and more fullness in the lips, tits, and hips, as Julian would say. They were each wearing office dress: Hickory wore a green skirt with white blouse, shoes, and hose while Sasha wore a red skirt with yellow blouse and black heels that had stars on them.

During the ambush on Radar, they were revealed to be true witches. That meant they were mostly TMs. But they each still wore chokers which Radar had used to keep them in line with aural suppression. No one was sure the chokers could be removed without blowing their heads off. The continued mark of the collar infuriated them.

Ted Bundt actually owned the office in the skyscraper that served as the headquarters of World Marine Casualty Insurance in Berlin. Ted was an average looking, middle-aged man of 57, with short-cut gray hair, sagging jowls, and lots of moles. He was wearing a very expensive black suit.

They all raced into the office within seconds of each other, all having been fortunately nearby.

"We move now," snapped Julie, adjusting the gloves on her right hand. Her onesie was perfect, as if painted onto her body.

"Where is Calico, by the by?" asked Julian.

"Searching for Staurvosky," said Julie, and she laughed.

It was not comforting sound.

"Jason?" called Calico, searching for Staurvosky. She had arrived with Quotient in the well-manicured backyard of his home in Kansas City. The trees were bare, and the leaves raked, the fenced-in yard ready for winter.

She moved to the house and found the door unlocked.

Broken.

"Damn," she hissed.

With Quotient hovering above her, she had no fear of the attacker still being on the premises. She moved inside a few steps and in the foyer found Staurvosky laying naked on the Aztec patterned rug lay over the tile floor. He was a collector of antique weapons, and someone had taken a sword from an Aztec collection and driven it through his back. Blood soaked the rug and stained the white walls.

Obviously, he was dead.

She frowned. Touching the blood, she realized it was warm.

Removing her phone, she called Englehart. "We have a complication. Staurvosky is dead, clearly murdered and recently."

"Murdered?" asked Englehart over a lot of background noise, as he was on the set of one of his shoots. "Are you certain?"

"He has a sword through his back. I doubt he backed into it accidentally," she said dryly.

"Well, I'm with you there. Recently?"

"The blood is still warm. I'm guessing within the hour."

"Calico . . . there's no one in Kansas City that could get to Staurvosky and murder him. He was a formidable TM. He could hold his own against even someone like you or Geneva Kane."

"I know," said Calico, her voice laced with concern. "But he's still dead."

"Let me get to my office. I'll call you back in about two minutes."

"Sure. Thank you."

Once she hung up, she put her phone on the end table in the foyer and looked at herself in the mirror. She looked old, gaunt, worried . . . and tired.

Then she used her phone to run some apps. She detected a massive tachyonic surge earlier, about the time she was on Mars breaking up the brawl between Trixie and Saunders but before arriving.

She entered the main home, which had the living room to the left and the bedrooms and bathrooms down a hallway to the right. She went right. Finding a small room that looked like a study, buried in books and disorganized folders, she saw Staurvosky did have a security system as she suspected.

Cuing up the footage from the morning wasn't difficult. Quickly, she saw him walk from the living room while eating an apple. Then the sword flew from off camera and killed him. The apple rolled into the living room.

There was no sign of an intruder.

Nor was there any sign of an intruder on any of the other cameras.

Englehart called and didn't even bother with a greeting. "I was thinking he probably has security."

"He does. It shows nothing. The sword flew from nowhere and hit him. The room with his collections is at the other end of the hall."

"No sign of other intruders?"

"None. I'm running a tachyon surge and aural detector program," said Calico, typing furiously on Staurvosky's computer. "It should take only seconds to run."

When it finished, Calico looked at the reading on the screen and gasped, "Oh, my God."

"What's wrong?"

"Tachyon surge levels *off the scale*. This was a portal or someone that can be a portal. *Damn her eyes!*" shouted Calico, rising and slamming her fist into the keyboard, breaking the 'r' key.

"Calico, who is it? What's wrong?"

"This signature is *unique!*" Then Calico was gone, instantly realizing the danger, instantly having Quotient return her to Red Kelkirkstadt.

Englehart simply stared at the ceiling, wondering what was going on, and looking very worried.

"I'm worried. Something is out of sync here," said Yellow.

Smith looked at her. They were in the monitoring station in Calico's room, a small room barely bigger than a closet that had two shelves with banks of monitors that covered the entire city.

"She's just sitting there," said Yellow, nodding towards Trixie sitting on the bed.

"So?"

Yellow turned left and looked up at him, for she was sitting in a swivel chair while he was standing. "So she just got chewed out and almost threatened with death. But she's not relaxing or afraid or doing anything? That seems weird."

He laughed. "All white people are weird."

She gave him a look. "This isn't the time for jokes."

Seriously, he said, "I can check on her in person."

Yellow nodded. "Do that."

Smith took less than a minute to reach Trixie's room. He knocked on the door and called through it. "Trixie? It's Smith. You okay?"

"Go away," she said sullenly. She had put on black boots and now was sitting on the bed with her head in her hands, because she had a terrible, terrible feeling that this was finally . . . going to be the end.

"Can we talk?"

"*Go the fuck away!*" she shouted, and she used TK to hurl a shoe into the door to emphasize her point.

"Sorry," said Smith. He then stepped back and used his cell to call Yellow.

"I saw her side. She's upset. I guess just . . . oh, fuck."

"What"

"She's vanished."

Chapter Thirteen
The Great Escape
November 16, 2020

"Where are we?" asked Trixie, moments after she threw up due to being abruptly portaled out of the main city.

"Far below the city," said Julie.

Trixie wiped her mouth on the hem of her shirt, then held up her phone for light.

"Oh!"

Trixie was shocked to see they were in a long, stone corridor that had a concrete floor but otherwise seemed to have been drilled at random and oddly without proper support. They walked to a door, Julie in the lead, then travelled down a long, seemingly endless spiral staircase that had been hidden behind the wall in the sub-basement of the city.

They descended seemingly forever. Trixie started counting stairs, gave up at 242, and they covered at least that many more. The spiral staircase was hewn of rock directly from the rock and was very rough. There was no light other than Trixie's phone. Julie didn't need light.

When they arrived at the bottom, they were on a large, unpolished cement floor, as if someone had thrown random blocks of cement together and pushed them into one mass. There was no exit. Trixie looked around and felt her heart in her chest.

"Is this . . . is this it for me?" she meekly asked, her voice cracking at the end.

Julie smiled darkly, amused by Trixie's fear. "It's not *your* end, if that's what you mean."

Then Julie turned and put her hands against the rock wall. It began to slowly melt away, revealing a metal brace creating a semi-doorframe. The molten rock pooled along the edges of the wall and cement floor. Now Trixie understood the floor. It was rough due to the repeated melting of the wall creating new rock beneath them.

"It's hot. Step quickly."

Trixie jumped over the puddle of molten rock at her feet and stepped in the chamber. Julie clapped her hands and suddenly there was light — dim light, but enough for Trixie to gasp and step back.

Julie saw the shock in Trixie and grabbed the redhead's arm, preventing her from stepping back into the rapidly cooling but still hot rock.

Before them was a *massive* underground chamber roughly the size of a football stadium. It had a similar shape — a dome and then a smooth, circular ceiling. There were a few stalagmites and stalactites scattered about, as well as random rock, but the floor was clearly manufactured concrete.

The striking feature was the far wall where there was a large, stone wall. The stones were embedded in concrete, but they were layered panels, some protruding, some recessed, and seemed to somehow create . . . faces. Faces of horror, as if the men and women on the rock were being executed at the time they were immortalized.

Waiting for them were Bundt, Julian, Sasha and Hickory, having been portaled here by Julie before she went to the city to retrieve Trixie.

"Who are these people?" asked Trixie in a scared whisper.

"This is our team: Trixie, meet Ted, Sasha, Hickory, and Julian."

"Uh, hi," said Trixie.

They all ignored her. Julian said to Julie, "We've marked the positions."

"Good. I anticipate Calico's arrival very soon. She's found Staurvosky's corpse. Assume the positions."

"What's going on?" asked Trixie, like a nerdy girl in high school kept out of the loop by mean girls.

Julie turned and folded her arms over her supple breasts and said seductively, "We need inside the graves. This is where we shall use the big, dumb floating puppy."

Trixie looked horrified. "*Quotient*? I can't help you with that!"

Julie laughed. "I know that. Stand by the door. If Yellow and Smith arrive before Calico, you must hold them off. Fail and you go to the island in Hell. Understood, wench?"

Horrified, Trixie nodded and took up a position by the door, shaking. Once she was in position, Julie moved to the others. "Are you ready?"

They all confirmed, some with nods, some with grunts. Julie smiled. She activated the lights in the chamber, very dull lights that made the whole chamber eerier, as if it were lit by the biggest candle in the world.

The chamber was a perfect square, and the four Germans had created the perfect square with their positions. Geometric channeling exponentially increased any type of channeling spell, and perfect shapes were the strongest. The strongest was the square. Julie stood near a bank of computers with huge dials, between the Germans and Trixie, who was guarding the door.

Julie snapped to them, "Be ready. We act very soon."

"We'll be there soon. I had no idea this stairwell existed," said Yellow. "It's not on the plans."

They had picked up Julie and Trixie on camera outside the massive underground chamber, but unable to portal, they had to meet the tunnel from a sewage tunnel and were several minutes behind.

"I gotta say, I have a bad feeling. Nothing about this is on the plans," said Smith.

"I'm with you there," she said glumly.

They continued descending, using their phones for light, yet still feeling completely in the dark.

"Sitting here doing nothing leaves me feeling in the dark," said Jen internally to Oscar, who was in control of their shared physical form. They were sitting on the bed in their room.

"Something's abnormal here," said Oscar, studying their phone. "I'm getting huge tachyonic surges from below the city."

An alarm suddenly blared like an air raid siren.

Jen raced for the door.

When she opened it, Calico was standing there looking horrified, Quotient floating above her. Instantly, Calico said, "I need your help to save everyone."

Chapter Fourteen
The Great Escape II
November 16, 2020

"She's coming!" shouted Julie at the team.

Then Julie moved to a position directly between Sasha and Julian, which put her facing the giant 'faces' on the far wall, the square between her and the far wall. Her position was in the precise center of the side of the square and created a precise distance match to the distance of the other side of the square to the far wall. Her spell was a basic geometric channeling spell.

Calico and Quotient suddenly materialized.

Calico had intended to materialize, as per her orders to Quotient, behind Julie. But that *didn't* happen. This was because Julie had created a massive tachyonic fissure in the chamber. Quotient acted instinctively and materialized where Julie left a tachyonic void, a place for a safe materialization.

Directly in the center of the square.

"*Geyarghhhhhhhhhhhhgggggggggggghhhhhhh!*" screamed Calico as the Germans instantly channeled the tachyonic force of Julie and Quotient into a power source.

Calico should have been incinerated by psychic heat. That had been Julie's intent. But Quotient instinctively recognized the danger and portal Calico out of the square.

She disappeared.

Julie shouted, "Ignore that. We have *him*. Focus! Focus! Channel his energy!

"*LET THE GREAT ESCAPE COMMENCCCCCCCCCCEEEEEEEEEEEE!*"

She ended by screaming as the room went pure yellow, as if the sun had landed in the square.

Trixie fell to the floor, screaming, covering her eyes with her hands and yet still being blinded. The Germans also fell back as the spell shot tachyons, psychic heat, and anti-matter at the wall of faces. The rock began to melt. As the Germans fell, the square lost its shape, but that didn't matter. The process was too far along to be halted.

The Four Cornered Wheel now held control of the entire spell, something normally impossible in a geometric spell. But the Four Cornered Wheel was an entity of great power — and having Quotient at the center of the spell also rewrote the rules of geometric channeling. With Quotient at the center of it, reduced to being the motor in the most powerful machine ever devised, the spell was nearly unstoppable.

In the stairwell, Yellow and Smith heard the commotion. As they raced down the final stairs, they found Calico huddled in a ball, shaking on the floor near the door.

When the blinding light surged, they all screamed and fell back, blinded, in agony.

Then it all stopped.

The silence was agonizing after the screams and noise of the tachyon and anti-matter surge. Quotient floated above them, nearly white, clearly depowered by the act. The rock across the chamber was covered in smoke and fog.

The Germans were all dead. They were pools of smoking tissue that had liquefied . . . their inability to hold the form of the square doomed them to death by psychic heat. This was not part of Julie's plan, but it wasn't an important complication. The Germans had no further role other than to service her needs. Now she would have plenty of toadies to fill that role.

Julie stood with fists at her side and a smug smile on her face. "It is done! The Great Escape commences in minutes."

"No!" shouted Calico, staggering out of the stairwell and collapsing on the floor near Trixie, who was still writhing in agony on the floor with her hands over her face.

Julie turned and snickered. "Who are *you* to tell your god no?"

Then, seeing Trixie, Julie frowned. "You annoy me. Your role is at an end."

Julie then waved her hand and Trixie caught on fire.

"*Yearghhhhhhhhhhhhhhhhhhhh!*" screamed Trixie as she burned alive, inexplicably and horrifyingly unable to put out the flames.

Instantly, Calico moved to channel air away from Trixie, to smother the fire as there was no water source available, and she couldn't get control of the fire itself. But she had no chance. The Four Cornered Wheel was using psychic heat leftover from the spell, for which there was no prevention.

Trixie burned alive, screaming in agony, as had her hundreds of victims.

Then her corpse liquefied.

Calico turned and threw up.

Julie laughed. "Soft stomach? Psychic heat has rather unpleasant effects on the human body. This is one of many, although I rather like this one. It's tidy."

Calico was on her hands and knees and she looked up and glared. "(&*&*."

Quotient didn't move.

Julie smiled. "Your toy is *my* toy now. Don't worry. You can have him back shortly, once the Great Escape commences."

"Great Escape?" asked Calico.

Julie snapped her fingers and Calico found herself kneeling before Julie, her hands at her sides, unable to move. Calico was beyond terrified and horrified.

"Oh, little Kelkirk, thank you for finding your toy. Without him, I could never have opened the tombs. They are psychically and tachyonicly sealed to prevent any of us from opening it."

"Us?" she asked.

"I . . . am Martian."

With that, Julie's body suddenly began to rot and dissolve at a fantastically accelerated rate as the tachyonic energy the Four Cornered Wheel had been using to animate Julie's body for three years vanished instantly.

Before Calico stood a being that was . . . light. It was as if a rainbow had been turned into a yarn ball and it continually moved and floating and phased.

"My . . . God," said Calico, still unable to move. "You're . . . beautiful."

"Yes," said a voice from behind Calico.

Calico couldn't turn, but she recognized Smith's voice. He walked into the room, speaking in the same oddly seductive and smooth manner as Julie always had after her possession.

Smith said, "This is our true form. We are entities of the spirit. We have no physical form. We must possess physical form to breed and advance our race."

"Breed?" asked Calico.

Smith laughed. "Yes. I cannot thank you enough, Miss Kelkirk. It was *vital* that man civilize Mars. Long ago . . . long, *long* ago . . . there were sentients here, humanoid creatures from a place called Cygnus Omega. But they rebelled and trapped us in the tombs, the only way to contain us — a massive tachyonic breach in space. But some of us escaped and sought refuge in other dimensions."

Smith suddenly passed out and Julie, somehow reassembled, now rubbed Calico's face gently, taunting her. Calico wanted to vomit or kill her, she didn't know which.

"When your father used his tachyonic influx spell in '17 to try and find Quotient using Julie's probability cloud influenced powers, it freed me. I was able to hide in her body and continue to engineer events to free Quotient, for I knew only he had the power to disrupt the matrix to permit the Great Escape."

"You were behind *all* of this? Steering us in the background?" she asked with utter horror.

Julie smiled. "*Yesssssss.* I made sure you found Quotient and made sure events happened that would cause you to settle Mars. And now . . . *now* we have thousands of people here to serve . . . to feed us and help us *breed.*"

"You'll kill us all?"

"Death is inevitable." Smith shrugged. "You are cattle."

"Saunders will stop you," said Calico.

Smith laughed. "Saunders will be an excellent tool. She will not die. Her power and knowledge will greatly advance our race." Then Smith's eyes narrowed. "As for you . . . in seconds the tombs will open. Your fate must wait."

Julie then turned away from her but remained close by to stand guard. The Four Cornered Wheel was now hosted in Smith, but easily able to animate Julie's corpse, as it had for the last three years.

Calico tried desperately to move, but she was helpless. Quotient was barely a foot above the floor, still white. She didn't know where Yellow was, and Saunders hadn't appeared as planned.

Calico realized she was well and truly doomed, as was her entire hope of saving mankind, if her one ally didn't come through.

It was a horrifyingly humbling moment.

Moving to the rock, which now was visible as a purely smooth rock wall, the faces obliterated, Smith raised his hands and shouted, his voice echoing through the chamber.

"*&*&%&*^&*%^*&^*((*!!!!!!!*"

From the rock, dozens of rainbow entities flew out and flew up to the city.

"No! No, *please!*" shouted Calico.

Smith ignored her.

In the city above, Daisy Nettles was taking a shower. She turned off the water and reached for a towel.

And then a Martian entity entered her.

And she died.

And one of the Four Cornered Wheel walked the planet of Mars . . . again.

Calico screamed as she realized everyone in the city was about to be possessed as Julie had been in '17 — murdered, destroyed.

She had done this.

She had brought them all here . . . had been used all along. Instead of saving the people of Red Kelkirkstadt, she had delivered them to an instant, agonizing death.

The thought of their deaths enraged her. She was so angry she was actually able to move a fist.

But that didn't help her.

However, something else caught her eye.

Quotient was turning yellow.

She looked at Julie. "I'll stop you, monster."

Julie laughed.

Chapter Fifteen
The Great Escape III
November 16, 2020

In the city, chaos erupted as the Martians began to possess the thousands brought to the city after the disruption in Portland. Those humans had their souls evicted from their bodies, bringing instant death. The Martians then animated the corpse, as the Four Cornered Wheel had done for years with Julie.

There was one they could not possess, for he was not human.

Radar.

On the opposite side of the city from where the Four Cornered Wheel and Calico were in combat, robot Radar sat in a padded leather chair in his room, linked to a direct access terminal which would allow him to active the defense protocol Calico had shown him earlier. He'd been doing some minor hacking, mostly trying to find the location of Carmine and the others that had been kidnapped back in June.

The instant he read the surge from the cavern below, he activated the program. He knew the defense unit, as Calico called it, would work.

But they had to move fast.

And that wasn't happening.

"Too damn long!" he muttered, slamming a fist on the computer console. "We're going to lose everything by a matter of seconds!"

"I can't rush this," said Jen to Oscar and Anissa, her body sitting in her room.

"Time isn't on our side," said Oscar with a curt response.

"I've no choice. If I mishandle this, we could wind up trapped in Quotient's mind forever."

Oscar had no response to that. But Anissa did.

"Uh, then let's do it right," she muttered.

They were in the park in Jen's head, but they had Patty contact Quotient to 'play' with him. She projected her thoughts. Jen wasn't a telepath, but Quotient was, and he-it recognized the thought pattern.

The park was just the swing set and sand, and around them was nothing but a pale, yellow haze that stretched to infinity. Jen, Oscar, Anissa, and Donnie were there. Donnie was dribbling his basketball. The other alters comprising Jen's multiple personality had retreated to the furthest depths of her subconscious.

Quotient was riding a swing with Patty, although not sitting on the swing itself, as he hovered over it and mimicked her movements.

"Can Patty handle this? She's a child?" said Oscar.

"That's why she can handle it," said Jen.

Suddenly, Patty jumped off the swing and ran to the adults. "Mommy! Mister Quotient says his mommy, that Miss Calico woman, is in big trouble. He wants us to help him!"

Jen smiled and looked at Oscar. "See?" Then she said to Patty, "We want to help him, too. *What does he want us to do*?"

Patty just extended her right hand towards Quotient and her left towards Jen. "We must merge, mommy. At least for a while. Quotient can put Mr. Radar's toys in the right place at the right time."

Julie stood over Calico and said, "I need just about two Earth minutes to release the last of the Martians. Then there will be *thousands*." She reached down and shoved Calico's head towards the ground and taunted her. "Then I will kill you and return you to the dust that made you."

Calico suddenly could move. She grabbed Julie's foot . . . or she tried to, but her hand swung right through it. Julie then kicked Calico in the face, then the ribs, then kicked her aside.

"You think yourself powerful, daughter of Kelkirk, but you are a meat-sack like all the rest. You are food. But you will not feed us. You are a scheming, intelligent meat-sack who is much less dangerous dead. Don't worry. Your death will be quick."

"Why wait?" asked Calico with a snarl, wiping blood from her nose.

Julie said nothing, but she was keeping Calico alive just in case Quotient were to be needed further. To Calico, she just smiled and said, "To make you fully appreciate your failure before you die."

Calico doubted that — she correctly suspected Julie feared a reaction from Quotient if she were murdered. But Calico didn't have much time to think about it.

The entire chamber shuddered.

Both women looked at Quotient, but while a more vibrant yellow, he hadn't moved. Then they looked up. Nothing.

Then they crashed like an avalanche through the wall that held the tombs, dozens of them, shattering the seemingly invincible rock and scattering the faces across the floor.

"No. *Nooooooooooooooooooo!*" shrieked Julie with horror.

"Good Lord," said Calico to herself breathlessly, so excited that she spoke out loud.

What happened next was shocking and fast. Radar had tried to activate the defenses, but that was going to be too slow. Quotient, however, through his telepathic link with Paty, was able to access the defenses and portal the defense unit. At least fifty gigantic figures broke through the seemingly impregnable rock of the tombs, scattering the disembodied Martian forms that were flying through the chamber like straws in a tornado, having been portaled to the chamber behind the rock by Quotient.

The army consisted of lizard-like creatures wearing armor. They were strange, man-like lizards with silver helmets, gauntlets, boots, and shiny metal guns. But unlike the Subject Seven creatures found in Canada by Jennifer Saunders in 2004,[5] these creatures were *gigantic*. They were at least fifteen feet tall and armed.

Critically, their weapons had an effect on the *disembodied* form of the Martians. The Subject Seven clones fired at the disembodied forms and the Martians writhed in torment, turned into solid dust, and collapsed.

Smith dove for cover as the Four Cornered Wheel let go of its control of his body. Calico was shocked, but only for a split-second, because she knew she suddenly had a chance to escape this mess.

Horrified and distracted, Julie let her control of Calico slip. Calico dove forward and tackled Julie by the legs and tried to grab Julie's face, but Julie blew her aside with a tachyonic surge. Calico was slammed into the far wall.

Knocked silly, Calico struggled to get to her feet as Julie stormed forward shrieking, *"YOU WILL PAY FOR DECEIVING US!"*

Radar suddenly appeared from the doorway, diving and tackling Julie — or at least, attempting to do so.

But he went right through her, and Julie continued her murderous advance.

Behind her, the Martians fled desperately, but no matter where they went, the Subject Seven army blew them apart. Their guns were not anything remotely normal. They fired tachyonic imprints and it followed the Martians as if on a homing beacon, cutting through solids to find them no matter where they fled. Then it disrupted their aural matrix, causing them to dissipate like ghosts fading in the morning sun.

The same happened throughout the city, except that in those cases the corpses of the human shells collapsed, then dissolved.

Julie shrieked, *"I will kill you, meat-sack!"*

As Julie raised her arms, Calico saw Quotient move behind her.

---

[5] Way back in the prelude to the TM series "Wendigo!"

Calico laughed.

Quotient suddenly struck. Julie shrieked and ungodly, horrific scream, as if she were a teenager being eaten alive by wolves.

"Mommy! Keep firing!" shouted Patty in the park.

They were aiming at a spot in the sky, but it wasn't the sun. It was the portal out of Quotient's amorphous body and targeting Julie.

Outside, Julie screamed as she was struck and began to dissolve, molecule by molecule.

"NOOOOOOOOO! NOOOOOOOOOOO! I MUST NOT DIE! THE GREAT ESCAPE MUST COMMENCEEEEEEEEEEEEEEE!

"THE GREAT . . . ESCAPE!

"THE GREAAAAAAAAAAAARRRRRRRRRRRRRRRRRRRRRRRRR!"

Then she was gone.

Radar raced to Calico's side and put out a hand. Calico unsteadily got to her feet and shouted, "We've got to account for all of them, and we've got to seal the tomb!"

"On it. Get Saunders out of Quotient," snapped Radar, running toward the far wall.

Calico was confused, but then she saw Saunders inexplicably dive out of Quotient's body as if she were emerging from a swimming pool.

"Good Lord," said Calico as Saunders landed at her feet, yellow waves of light radiating off her like heat.

Startled, Jen looked around. "Where am I?"

"In danger!" shouted Calico, grabbing Jen by the arm and dragging her for the door. She shoved Jen out the door, then turned to find Smith waking up.

"What hit me?" he asked groggily.

Calico crouched down, her feet standing on the liquified corpse of Trixie, but she didn't notice. "Hurry. Get out."

Smith stumbled to the door, and Jen helped pull him though.

Calico said, "This is my job now. Stay here. I've got to destroy this place."

Then she slammed the door shut.

Turning, she saw Radar racing forward. "By my count, based on this app, we're too late. Nearly every human in the city is possessed. It's 97% saturation, and I don't know if these lizard things can kill them all."

Calico felt as if she had been raped. "Oh, my God."

"We have to blow up the entire city. Is that possible?"

She nodded. "The city was built on an alien-ship, and it has an anti-matter destruct. It will vaporize the entire canyon until the anti-matter dissipates."

"That'll sure the fuck do it. How do we turn it on?" asked Radar.

Calico removed her phone. "I can configure to avoid this room. Get the others outside and pull them in."

Radar suddenly opened the door and grabbed Jen and shouted at Yellow and Smith, "Inside, now!"

They raced inside and Radar shut the door.

Calico was pale with shock and fear, but she said to Quotient, "*&(&(*!" Then she said to the others, "I've ordered him to protect us. I don't have time to reconfigure the app."

"Huh?" said Smith.

Calico ignored him and pressed the app.

Far, far below Red Kelkirkstadt in the core of the ship that was the size of several ocean liners, a tiny red button lit up. Several ionic rays turned off.

Anti-matter raced forward, dissipating everything in its path.

Except the chamber where Quotient protected Calico, Yellow, Smith, robot Radar, and Jennifer Saunders.

In Jen, Oscar realized with horror what was happening. Taking command of Jen's body, he shouted, "Calico, no! Everyone will die!"

Calico shrieked, "They're already dead. They're *all* possessed!"

Then there was a horrendous shaking for nine seconds as some of the structures dissolved.

And then it was dead silent.

Red Kelkirkstadt by Douglas Todt

Chapter Sixteen
Devastation
November 16, 2020

"Is it . . . is it over?" Jen asked Radar.

"For now. Unless she wants to kill us," said Radar nodding towards Calico.

Stunned, horrified, grieving, Calico knelt before the puddle of ooze that had been Trixie Taylor.

"What . . . what happened?" whispered Yellow.

Calico fell to her knees and said, "We . . . have lost. The city is destroyed."

Jen looked at Radar. "Those things. I saw tiny version of them in Canada, years ago!"[6]

"Yeah, Subject Seven. It's a long story, Jen, but basically the Consortium got hold of samples and cloned them. I'll give you more details later," said Radar.

Calico sat on her knees, staring at the ground.

Jen approached from behind. Quotient moved to a defensive position.

Jen said, "Calico . . . we don't want to hurt you. Let this end."

Calico turned and looked at Jen with tears in her eyes. "It wasn't supposed to be like this . . . this is a nightmare."

---

[6] Way back in the second prelude novel "Wendigo!" (2004)

Quotient was shuddering, and said something similar to, "*(^*&^**" But they all heard it in their heads instead of verbally.

Jen was cautious, taking the lead, Radar well back.

"Calico, we're the only ones left here. Are you . . . can we end this? Can we all go back to Earth?"

Slowly, as if rising from the grave, Calico forced herself to her feet. Her grief was agonizing. All of her hopes and dreams had been reduced to puddles of ooze by the Four Cornered Wheel. It had used her from the start. Her dream was shattered. She had never felt like this, not when her mother died, not when Keith died. She felt raped. That was the only context she had for this raw, aching pain.

She turned and said to Jen, "This is a . . . disaster. We can never settle here now. We don't know how many . . . entities . . . like the Four Cornered Wheel exist."

"I would agree," said Jen, parroting words from Oscar, who was listening internally keenly.

Calico had no fear of attack. She had no belief that Jen or Radar could harm Quotient in any manner, no matter how Saunders had worked with Quotient, and also knew they were unlikely to try anything since Quotient was their only hope of returning to Earth and avoiding a slow death on Mars. She looked past Jen at Radar and said, "You knew about this. You were working with the Germans, faked your own death at Julie's hands."

"Yeah, I knew something about this, Miss Kelkirk," said Radar, choosing deliberately to be subservient and not his normal cocky, brash self. He had no desire to live out a long, painful life on Mars all alone locked in a robot body that couldn't die.

"Something?"

"I'm a seer. I was stuck in the parallel dimension with Jen here. Not by choice. When there, I foresaw a danger that would merge the universes. That danger may not be over. But the first step in that was the Four Cornered Wheel succeeding. We've *stopped* that." He paused and said, "And I suspect the rest . . . is up to you."

"We don't want war. Your dream is over." Jen put out a hand. Like Radar, she knew the desperation of their situation, but she also recognized Calico's grief. "Calico, let's work together."

Calico was ignoring her completely, her gaze fixed on robot Radar. "If you are a seer, what happened that changed your visions? What was the catalyst?"

Radar wasn't sure why she was asking, but he saw no harm in answering either. "Me. No one saw me coming. No one could factor me into any of their projected plans because no one even knew I existed, let alone could be a source of interference. And even if someone had known I was alive in the parallel world, there was supposedly no access. No one would factor me into plans."

"Not even the Four Cornered Wheel," said Calico thoughtfully. Then she picked up on something he had said. "What do you mean, the latter part is up to me?"

Radar studied her and saw fear, anger, and pain in her face. He recognized she was in a fragile emotional state, and he also knew he damn well had better keep her on his side or he and Saunders were in for a long, lingering death.

Cautiously, he said, "You know that tachyon displacement accelerates global warming. It's been known for a few years now that the portal and space gems used by Zenith, Lexx, and others have accelerated global warming by releasing psychic heat, which doesn't dissipate."

She nodded curly, conveying understanding and impatience.

He paused. "Understand I just came back to Earth, this Earth, in May. I took a position undercover using Bundt and Julian as toadies, and my objective there was to ferret out the Four Cornered Wheel, though I didn't know precisely that she was the entity at the time, but that was obvious to me when she showed up right about when I took over Bundt's insurance operation." He paused. He could see both Calico and Saunders were giving him intense attention. "Once I had access to their operation, I had access to a lot of Consortium documents that you don't know about, Calico."

She glared. "Go on."

"One is Sigurdsson's research into global warming, though I gather a lot of his information is really based on the work by that guy Milgrom. But there's key information in there that, besides the stressors on global warming, all this movement is breaking down dimensional barriers as well. That probably explains how Zenith got her start zapping across worlds in the first place back in '04, not just having a portal gem. And how Tripper and Geneva got zapped to and back from Hell so easily, for another example."

"Pure assumption, but I'm listening," said Calico with a dark and worried look.

"Anyhow, your bubble toy there," said Radar, nodding at Quotient, "is unleashing tachyons at an *alarming* rate. It's entirely possible *he* has *near-fatally* weakened the barriers between dimensions. And if those barriers continue to fail . . . well, there goes the ballgame."

There was silence, for all parties immediately understood the implication. If the barriers between dimensions fell, they would all merge in cataclysmic fashion. Most likely nothing would survive.

Calico finally said, "This is theoretical."

"Somewhat. The numbers correlate, but I didn't see anything in the work proving Quotient's damage is permanent or irreversible."

"This means nothing," said Calico. "What matters is the fact before us. Mars cannot save mankind. I must find other solutions."

"Using Quotient?" asked Radar.

"Using whatever is necessary." She looked at Saunders. "You understand, correct?"

Jen just nodded, as encouraged by Oscar.

Calico turned to Jen. "Clegg, it seems your offer of aid is no longer feasible, since we no longer have a planet to move to."

Shaking her head, Jen felt Oscar slip into control of her body. When Jen had first become a 'soul' survivor, she fought this vigorously, and even when she allowed it, the process was difficult. But now it was as natural and simple as changing clothes.

"No, Miss Kelkirk," said Oscar-Jen. "You no longer have Mars. But we can explore other planets, be they in this dimension . . . or in others."

Calico snapped a look at her. "You would propose to continue your aid?"

"Of course."

Calico frowned. "Logistically, this is now somewhat more complicated. I do not believe anyone to be safe on Mars now, nor would I know where to settle. The key to the Mars settlement was the spacecraft being here, enabling us to build around it before Quotient was found, as it had a ready-made power source."

"With that, I *completely* concur," said Oscar-Jen emphatically.

Calico looked up at Quotient and clearly *asked,* ")()(*^&$$?"

")&*&()*(."

Calico looked at Radar. "Quotient is sufficiently powered to return us all to Earth. Miss Saunders . . . for the moment, I will return you to your allies. I have to arrange secure facilities if we are to work together."

"I understand," said Oscar-Jen.

"Wonderful. We will now go."

"Uh, thanks," said Radar.

Then they were gone.

They appeared in a grassy field with a large building in the background that looked like a prison, then suddenly Radar and Jen moved again.

They materialized with Quotient in the middle of the desert.

Then Quotient vanished.

Radar looked at Jen. "Well . . . he didn't eat our souls. I guess that's something."

At this point, Oscar said internally to Jen, "That was exhausting. Can you assume control?"

"Certainly," said Jen, and once again Jennifer Saunders controlled her own body. She looked around. "Uh, where are we?"

Radar pointed. "That's an highway over there, and I see an Arco sign. Calico probably didn't want him to materialize us anywhere near a population and draw attention. It's not far. Let's find out."

They walked across the desert sand. Jen said, "Those aliens up there, not the Martians, the lizard soldiers. How did she get ahold of Subject Seven? I thought the only one that landed we, uh, well . . . we kind of killed him by accident in Canada."

"I don't know the details. I don't know how Calico got hold of them, but she did," said Radar thoughtfully. "Then she used CRISPR to genetically modify them — well, I say 'she,' but it was probably Kosar or one of their scientists. That kind of genetic manipulation isn't Calico's field at all." He shrugged. "We'll probably never know the full details. Anyhow, the key was Quotient portaling them from Earth to Mars and arming them with remnants of his own tachyonic composition. The Martians had no chance to combat that."

As Jen knew, CRISPR was a way to rewrite DNA. Scientists at Osaka University in Japan in the 1980s had noticed unusual and repeated DNA sequences next to a gene they were studying in a common bacteria. The sequences were part of a sophisticated immune system that bacteria use to fight viruses. And that system, whose very existence was unknown until 2007, eventually provided scientists with power to rewrite the code of life — discovering that the bacterial system can be harnessed to make precise changes to the DNA of humans, as well as other animals and plants.

Of course, what neither of them knew was that the Consortium had received the tissue samples of Subject Seven, collected by Jen's team in Canada in 2004 for research, from Grant and Jameson in an information exchange in 2016.

"That's a little nerve wracking," said Jen.

"Yeah. Makes you wonder if she's modified other life-forms."

They were silent for a time, each contemplating the new danger that would pose for everyone. There was a sign about a mile away. She asked Radar, "What did you make of her reaction?"

"I dunno."

Jen frowned. "I'm a little worried when I talked about other planets . . . it seemed like that thought hadn't occurred to her. I might have opened a can of worms there."

"Nah, I don't think so. She was just in shock from the destruction of her plan. They've been working on this for years, remember. This was her moment of utter triumph and instead it became utter failure, and she's not really used to failure. I think she was just reacting to the thought that there were other options, or the fact you still wanted to work with her, desperate for something to cling to."

"I will try to work with her, Radar. She still has Quotient," said Jen.

"Yeah." They walked for a moment, and then Radar added, "I don't know if she'll recruit you again. I think she has a lot to think about."

"So do we. The Four Cornered Wheel destroyed her plan and her soldiers, but she still has Quotient and her allies and the portal gems. She can do a lot of damage. And she'll never stop, because she's convinced she's the savior of the world."

Radar said, "Which she isn't. She isn't the savior of the world or humanity. She just wants to set up her own kingdom and present it as that."

Jen stopped. "I don't think it's that simple, Radar. I really don't. She's convinced the cataclysm is here and escape is the only hope. And she may be right."

Radar nodded. "Well, let's hope not." He clapped his hands. "At least with the Germans and Julie, so to speak, dead meat, I can slip right back into control of Bundt's financial operation. That will help us a lot." He paused. "But if you're right, Calico's also back to work. She's probably at home setting plans in motion right now."

Calico arrived in her home in Germany. She said to Yellow, Smith and Quotient, "You may stay or have Quotient take you somewhere, but I must rest."

"We'll be in the guest quarters," said Yellow. "I'll . . . seal off Trixie's room."

"Please."

They exited, stunned and grieving. Calcio went to her room and immediately into the shower and took a long, hot shower. She exited the shower, combed her long, straight hair.

Then she fell to the floor and began sobbing wretchedly, letting out all the emotion pent up from the battle and destruction of Red Kelkirkstadt. Like a marionette with the strings cut, she was suddenly too weak to even move or walk. Huddled in the fetal position, naked on the cold tile, she sobbed and sobbed and sobbed for quite some time. It felt like hours, but it was only perhaps fifteen minutes.

Suddenly, Quotient materialized above her.

"*(&." Her voice was somber.

"*(&*&," expressed Quotient.

Calico forced herself to her knees and said, "*(&*."

Quotient vanished.

Her body suddenly seemed to weigh more than it would on Jupiter. She used the toilet as a steadying tool and pulled herself to her feet. Exhausted, she made her way to the towel rack on the wall and removed her blue robe. Putting that on, she cinched it with a white belt and stumbled into the main hallway. She made her way to the kitchen, which was very sterile — all black and white cabinets with a marble countertop and stainless-steel appliances. She sat at a square, black table.

Seconds later, Yellow and Smith entered, also having showered. All three of them were as somber as pallbearers.

"What now?" asked Smith.

"Red Kelkirkstadt is dead," said Calico softly, "but saving the human race is a project that is far, far from over."

Chapter Seventeen
Lessons Learned

"Nothing. I've heard nothing from Calico," said Jen a week later, sitting glumly in Little Jack's office. She wore a pink sweatshirt over a white collared shirt, jeans, and sneakers, and was leaning her head on her hands. Little Jack wore his typical pin-striped shirt and jeans combination.

"Yeah. Everything has gone very quiet. I guess we can assume that plan is a bust," said Little Jack, eating an Egg McMuffin from McDonald's. The sun was just coming up.

"Any news from Geneva?" asked Jen per an internal request from Oscar.

Little Jack shook his head. "No. After Carerra contacted them and they were ambushed in Egypt, she went back to Siberia to work with Golden Bear and a Russian team. Even if Carerra wasn't being truthful, and all indications are she is a double-agent and was, being tracked so easily to Cairo makes bringing in any outsiders risky. We don't want to recreate that mess we had with Carmine and our other information sources getting kidnapped."

Jen nodded. "That was not a good thing."

Little Jack grimaced and said, "It's . . . well, it's worse than you think. Radar let me know that when he hacked the Red Kelkirkstadt computers, one of the items he found was the city's register. Our friends all died there, all consumed by the Martians — based on what you've said.

Jen looked very sad. "Yes . . . yes, there were no survivors in the city. Radar found no life signs. And the bodies . . . dissipated. Oh, gosh."

"Yeah," said Little Jack, then he rubbed his eyes. "I'm notifying families, where that applies. Where it doesn't, well, people like Carmine had no family." He shook his head. "At least Searly's parents have been looking after his dog. For people like Kuss' wife and child, well, it's gonna be a difficult explanation."

Jen shook her head. "We have to stop this before more of us get killed."

Little Jack nodded. "I know."

"So . . . so, what now?"

"Geneva and Golden Bear are working in Siberia. Colin and Medina are headed back to Europe to work on finding a way to get Mary out of her coma and help Radar keep an eye on what's going on there. Radar says his precognition has changed considerably, but he can't figure it out, and wants them in the area in case he needs to move fast."

"Where's everyone else?"

"Thunder, Ashley, and Searly continue to help in Portland, using Ashley's parents' home in Centralia as an unofficial base. Tripper is still wiped out from saving them in Portland. He's as safe there as anywhere. Sly is stationed here in case I need a field agent in an emergency. Sam is basically out of action, staying with Mark Meachum and Theresa, who is still on leave after that whole animal park problem, in Stark. Jameson is off doing undercover stuff. Sylvester is working his sources . . . Joy is still my girlfriend. I leave anyone out?"

Jen smiled. "I don't think so."

Then Little Jack grinned. "So, you got Quotient to work with you?"

She smiled an unusual and surprisingly wicked smile. "Patty did, yes. I think if I get around him again, Paty can wrest control . . . or even convince him to help us."

"Then we gotta try it. If what Radar says is right about Quotient's tachyonic surges causing dimensional rupture, fuck, as bad was what we had it with him eating souls is nothing. He could cause massive destruction if Calico keeps using him."

"Which she will."

"I don't think she'll work with you. So, we've got to somehow find another way to get you near Quotient again."

She nodded. "We'll work on it."

He nodded, but glumly.

Jen frowned. "Basically, our problem is the same as it was. Calico still has Quotient and even if she can't move people to Mars, she can devise some other plan. She won't stop. She's obsessed . . . rightfully so, I guess."

"What do you mean?"

"She's saving the world. How can you do that if you're not obsessed?"

Chapter Eighteen
The Final Solution

Calico stumbled to her waterbed, the only light in the room from the lights over the aquarium and a small LED digital clock in the far corner. The result was somber and eerie.

Still nude and wet, she lay on her back, hands over her face, coming to grips with the catastrophic events on Red Kelkirkstadt.

Everyone had died.

Everything had been destroyed.

Everything she had worked for the last few years had gone up in just *minutes*.

She felt *raped*. She *had* been raped, emotionally at any rate, by the Four Cornered Wheel. It had manipulated her for its own ends, then brutally violated her by stealing her city and killing everyone.

Defeating it brought her no solace.

Her humiliation was supreme. She had been used and cast aside, and now . . . everyone would pay for her mistake. Humanity itself might well pay for her mistake, if the other plans, like those of the Quartet, didn't pan out either.

Slowly, she slid to the edge of the bed and sat. The only sound was the bubbling from the aquarium. It was silent and somber, as was she.

And on top of it all, she had failed and disgraced her family, her father. He had instigated the plan. It was her duty to carry it out, to bring the family and her wonderful father the honor life had denied him. And she had damn well fucked that up as well.

She went to her bureau, one of the few pieces of furniture as most of the room was given to aquariums, and opened the top drawer. There was a .33 inside.

Slowly, she took it out and loaded it.

"No!"

Stunned, she turned to find Englehart racing towards her, Quotient hovering above him. Intent on finishing her failure, she hadn't even noticed the yellow glow of Quotient's materialization — her body also partially blocked the light.

Before she could protest or raise the gun, Englehart grabbed her hand and ripped it away, tossing it backwards onto the bed. He was wearing a red and yellow Hawaiian shirt, white shorts, and brown flip-flops.

Once she was disarmed, she collapsed.

Englehart quickly dragged her towards the bed, pushing the gun to the floor, as Quotient watched. Calico needed only moments to begin to awaken. She was on her back. Englehart sat to her right on the bed, hovering over her.

"Calico? Can you hear me, dear?"

Slowly, she nodded and said, "Englehart. How?"

"Quotient simply showed up and took me. Thank the good Lord I was home and not, say, driving down the 101."

She didn't smile. "How . . . did he know?"

"You know he is sentient."

"&*^(^$$*," said Quotient.

Calico said gently, "!!!&."

Quotient disappeared.

Englehart said, "You sent him away?"

Gently, softly, she said, "I asked him to check on Yellow and Smith. They may . . . it's all done, Englehart. Destroyed."

His eyes widened. "What?"

Then she balled her fists and stared shrieking as if she were insane, screaming at the top of her lungs, nails cutting her hands, turning purple because she screamed so much she wasn't breathing. Englehart had no idea what to do. He held her shoulders, kept her pinned to the bed, and hoped to God she hadn't snapped and didn't attack him. He'd never hold her off.

But she suddenly stopped and started breathing deeply.

"Calico . . . what in the name of God happened?"

"God had nothing to do with it . . . nothing."

"Is . . . please, tell me what happened?" he asked. Nothing he could think of could drive her to suicide. Nothing.

But he couldn't think of what happened on Red Kelkirkstadt, not even with his writer's imagination.

Finally, Calico said, "Please, just let me die, like a true friend. Just let it end."

"I cannot do that."

She shut her eyes and sighed. "You don't know the pain."

"The pain of loss? You know better than that, dear. You know how I lost my wife and son."

This struck a chord in her. Slowly, she opened her eyes and said, "Englehart, I lost it all . . . all . . . I was a pawn *all along.*"

"I don't understand," he said. These were some of the hardest minutes of his life, trying to talk her down, figure out what happened, and knowing at any minute if she snapped and attacked him, he would likely die.

He was a very strong and clever man, misguided as he was.

That saved them both.

She looked him in the eyes. Her voice was soft, barely audible. She finally coughed and said, "You recall . . . Julie Julian."

"Yes."

Then Calico relayed a very abbreviated version of events. Englehart let her talk without asking questions, able to follow along and not interested in detail. While Calico was talking, he was getting information and she was calming down.

She closed by saying, "I had . . . Saunders and Radar sent home. That was probably . . . a mistake. But I couldn't . . . I'm not a killer. I couldn't kill them after they saved me . . . saved everyone from the Martians."

"That was a good thing. We bear them no anonymity, and . . . our plan seems, like these recent scripts reviewed by my drunken sot of a script editor, to need reworking."

Surprised, she looked at him with wet eyes and said hoarsely, "My friend, we can't. To settle another planet . . . we can't go to Mars after that anyhow . . . but the resources. Quotient can't sustain it, you know that. The ship on Mars was the whole point. That made it self-sustaining."

"There have to be other planets with ships, dear, and regardless the Quartet has their plan." He knew neither of them were convinced or pleased with the Quartet's plan, but he was throwing out anything to give her a lifeline of hope.

Calico hung her head. With disgrace, she said, "The Four Cornered Wheel used me, Englehart, used father, used us like lackeys. I am ashamed, humiliated, embarrassed, and guilty of the deaths of everyone on Mars. They were under my protection."

He grabbed her by the shoulders, and she looked at him. He said, "Those feelings are understandable. But you should not feel guilty. The Martians killed those people, not you. You were trying to save the world. It is not a task one can undertake without risks. Your father knew that. I know that. And you know that."

Barely a whisper, she said, "I am so ashamed. I was so stupid."

"No, you were tricked by an entity that seems to survive by tricking other physical entities."

Gently, he rubbed her cheek like a father with a daughter, though that wasn't quite their relationship. What they had was very hard to define, but it was very intense, intimate, and strong.

"Calico . . . do you remember the rage you felt when Keith was murdered?"

Pleased, he saw her face harden and anger in her eyes as she said, "Yes, of course. It is not something one ever forgets, having a lover murdered."

"That is what you must bring to the surface now. The Four Cornered Wheel is dead. To surrender now gives it victory. We must save mankind or all the deaths so far, all the things Quotient has done, are for nothing. We simply cannot give up now. *You* cannot give up now. We've lost Karla. Trixie. We can't lose anyone else." Then he started to cry and hugged her. "In the name of God, Calico, I can't lose you."

She sobbed, as did he.

They heled each other a long, long time. Finally, Calico said, "I am so glad you are here. Can you remain for a time?"

He broke the embrace, smiled, and said, "Of course, my dear one. I will be with you . . . until you are strong again."

And he was.

Very few men could have done what John Englehart did on this day.

Whether what he did was for good or ill . . . depends on what one feels about what happened *next*.